P9-EJI-886

AWAY WITH THE MANGER

A SPIRITUALLY CORRECT CHRISTMAS STORY

CHRIS FABRY

InterVarsity Press
Downers Grove, Illinois

InterVarsity Press® is the book-publishing division of InterVarsity Christian Fellowship®, a student movement active on campus at hundreds of universities, colleges and schools of nursing in the United States of America, and a member movement of the International Fellowship of Evangelical Students. For information about local and regional activities, write Public Relations Dept., InterVarsity Christian Fellowship, 6400 Schroeder Rd., P.O. Box 7895, Madison, WI 53707-7895.

Published in association with the literary agency of Alive Communications, Inc., 1465 Kelly Johnson Blvd., Suite 320, Colorado Springs, Colorado 80920.

This is a work of fiction. The characters and setting are products of the author's imagination. Any similarity to actual places or living people is entirely coincidental. The Spirit of Christmas, however, is real.

Cover illustration: Kurt Mitchell
Illuminated letters: Don Frye

ISBN 0-8308-1962-2

Printed in the United States of America ♾

Library of Congress Cataloging-in-Publication Data

Fabry, Chris, 1961-
    Away with the manger: a spiritually correct Christmas story/
    Christopher H. Fabry.
        p.   cm.
    ISBN 0-8308-1962-2 (cloth: alk. paper)
    I. Title.
PS3556.A26A9   1996
813'.54—dc20   96-16814
                                                     CIP

15	14	13	12	11	10	9	8	7	6	5	4	3	2	1
08	07	06	05	04	03	02	01	00	99	98	97	96		

To Reagan Michael
on your first Christmas

"Subscriptions went up, tolerance went down, and I don't want to talk about my blood pressure."

BETTY STANTON, PUBLISHER, *HARTVILLE DAILY NEWS*

"These people need to get over their love affair with the manger."

DIERDRA BERGMAN FREEP, PRESIDENT,
ATHEISTS AGAINST MANGERS

"In the Old Testament, God spoke from a bush, in a cloud and even through a donkey. This year he surprised us all and used Jackson Grim."

THE REVEREND MARTY KARLSEN, PASTOR,
HARTVILLE COMMUNITY CHURCH

"What do you want, Mary? . . . You want the moon?"

GEORGE BAILEY, *IT'S A WONDERFUL LIFE*

Introduction

The truth is, it was just one column. Nothing extraordinary. Every day I write one, hand it to the editor and move on to the next. I never expected what happened, but then who can predict such things?

I still don't know who sent that first letter with the song. It could have been one of those crazy fundamentalists. Judging from what happened to our town, it could have been an angel. I think the whole thing was like a saucepan filled with too much popcorn. It was only a matter of time before the lid blew off, and I just happened to be the one holding on when it did.

I was accused of many things during that Christmas season. The religious right said I was a liberal with an agenda. The local atheist, Dierdra Bergman Freep, branded me a closet conservative trying to impose my values. There were a few who thought I was a congenital liar and had made the whole thing up just to be ornery or to sell papers.

The facts are simple. I found a good letter with a humorous

song, and I was staring at a deadline. Period. No agenda. I wasn't fishing for an award. I just had a column to write.

I suspect it's the same feeling a mother gets when the cupboards are bare and her husband and kids show up hungry for dinner. You make the most with what you've got. That's all I did.

So I wrote the column, and believe me, this town hasn't been the same. That year we argued over the establishment clause and debated the lemon test. We had no idea how much words can affect a town. Now we do.

I never thought of myself as anything but a columnist, so I was surprised when they asked me to tell this story in a book. Most folks couldn't find Hartville on a map if you circled it for them, and we're so small I doubt if we would go through half the first printing of this book if each family bought ten copies. But I suppose publishers know more about things like that than I do.

I would like to thank Hartville Radio for their help in recreating transcripts from certain broadcasts, and the creative writers who penned the alternate Christmas song texts.

And I wish to thank the Snuggle Slipper Factory.

Jackson Grim
Columnist, Hartville Daily News

1
THE LETTER

 was crawling out from under the mail after Thanksgiving, wishing I hadn't taken those two days off. I always gain twenty pounds and do twice the work the next week to catch up. Plus, it takes me at least a month to get the turkey smell off my hands, and then it's time for Christmas, when we do it all over again.

I had twenty letters on the desk that morning, not counting junk mail. Five were from irate Hartville Cablevision customers complaining about my lighthearted column on the recent channel change. I interviewed "The Cable Fairy" in the column. I thought it was pretty creative, but for some reason changing channels on these people throws their life into a tailspin. One day they're watching the Home Shopping Network and the next it's ESPN, and they don't know what to do.

I filed those letters and moved on to the other hate mail from gun owners, religious wackos and fans of a certain talk radio host who shall remain nameless. It was a pretty ordinary stack.

Then I saw a letter addressed to "The Columnist." There was

no return address, and it didn't have postage. I figured someone had dropped it in interoffice mail. Could have been anybody inside or outside the paper.

I held it up to the light to check for plastic explosives. You can't be too careful these days. It looked clean, so I opened it.

Here's what I saw:

November 27

To The Columnist

Hartville Daily News

I am responding to your article concerning the City Council's decisions to ban and then marginalize our manger scene. As you may know, the crèche display is a tradition in our town that spans some decades. For more than fifty years Hartville has enjoyed a simple scene with a stable, animals, some shepherds, Mary, Joseph and the baby Jesus on the lawn in front of the city building. For some reason this scene has become offensive to a few. Though it is a replication of an historical occurrence supported by eyewitness accounts, it is not politically correct. This decision is supposedly for the good of all Hartville.

In a conciliatory effort by the council, in accordance with court rulings, it was decided that citizens can display the crèche only if we mix it with a variety of other symbols that celebrate the "Winter Holiday." This would mean Santa, the reindeer, snowmen (or snowpersons) and a host of other frolicking replicas that have nothing to do with the true meaning of Christmas.

Furthermore, the annual Christmas musical put on by the children of our schools has been stripped of songs that have "religious content." They will, however, be able to play such tunes if they are instrumental renderings.

In celebration of this action by our city, I have come upon

an alternative to a beloved Christmas song that children around the world enjoy at this time of year. I offer it in honor of the wise persons who have come up with this brilliant plan and hope the children of Hartville Elementary will be allowed to sing it during their program.

The song is entitled "Away With the Manger."

Away with the manger, we just don't have room,
We've got enough tinsel and big red costumes.
We'd like to hear music that goes with the day,
But if you sing words we'll make you go away.

We like all the snow and wreaths on the doors,
We love Christmas sales at department stores.
We want to rejoice in our good winter cheer,
So keep your religion, it's "X"mas this year.

Away with the manger, the menorah as well.
We love the old fat guy with presents to tell
The story of Christmas our culture holds dear,
To buy it on credit, no int'rest till next year.

Okay, you can have your display this year,
Just include a Frosty and all eight reindeer.
We'll put up a tree too, the rules we can bend,
We've got equal opportunity rights to offend.

Away with the manger, we've got a complaint,
Someone took issue with old Nick, that dear saint.
Be glad and be happy, you're not in the lurch,
You can sing of that baby next week in your church.

Signed,

Concerned in Hartville

I took one look at the letter and thought it was a gift from the gods. Perfect! In a column just before Thanksgiving I had agreed with the city fathers regarding the separation of church and state and thought their solution was a good one. But this was just too funny to risk losing in the great chasm known as "Letters to the Editor."

I quickly wrote some commentary around the letter and placed it in the bin on the desk of my boss, Betty Stanton.

Realize that Betty had not questioned a column of mine in at least two weeks—I think the last one had been the infamous stoplight installation piece. We don't see eye to eye on much of anything. Her life revolves around the paper and Elvis. She has one of those velvet wall hangings of the King in her office and a replica of his rhinestone-studded jumpsuit on her desk. Once I made a joke about Elvis's sideburns while he was still with us, and for a moment I thought I wasn't going to be. Betty's so devoted she made a pilgrimage to Graceland and brought back a signed copy of the single "Teddy Bear." She even calls her basement "the Jungle Room"—I've never had the nerve to actually visit.

Betty does respect my right to an opinion. She encourages my writing on controversial subjects, as long as they don't have anything to do with the King, thank you very much.

Later that day Betty walked into my office holding my column against her hip. She is not slight in stature. I could tell it was her by the great creaking of the concrete slab. Betty looked like a backhoe ready to tear the top off a condemned building.

"What is this?" she said.

"It's called a column, Betty. You know, about 750 words. They put that in the paper and people read it."

She was not amused.

"Where did you get the letter?"

"It was in the mail."

"Who's it from?"

"It wasn't signed."

I could tell she was pretty upset because she wasn't making small talk. Usually Betty beats around the bush with her conversation. Even if she were going to fire you, she'd start out by talking about how good the fruitcake was at the office party last year or offer you a peanut-butter ball, complete with the recipe. Underneath all those layers of Little Debbie cakes and Ho-Hos she keeps in her desk, she's a kind woman with a big heart.

But she wasn't in the mood for such conversation, and I'll admit I started questioning my judgment. I hadn't really thought about the piece that much. It had been reflex: I read, I laughed, I typed.

"What's the matter with it?" I said. "Some kind of legal problem?"

Betty took off her glasses with her free hand and let them dangle around her neck on their elastic cord. They're those black cat-eye glasses that went out of style about a hundred years ago, and I've wanted to take them off and crush them more than a few times. They left two blotches on her nose and crimson lines running straight back to her ears that looked like you could plant corn in them and get a pretty good crop.

The pupils of her eyes were as big as a pair of pine needles, and you would have thought by the way she looked at me that I had thrown her cat, Priscilla, in the blender and set it to purée.

"You know what people are going to say when they read this?" she said. Her chin, the top one, was all tight and puckered.

"I hope they laugh and say you ought to give me a raise, Betty."
She didn't return my smile.

"You're going to stir up more than you think if we print this."

"Aw, Betty, you're overdoing it. It's a letter. It's opinion. It's just a column. I've heard you say half the town takes the paper to make people think they can read and the other half only checks the obituaries to make sure they're not dead yet."

She put her glasses back on, and the blotches and lines disappeared.

"Don't say I didn't warn you," she said. I heard the sound of polyester in pain as she swished back down the hall. It was like the crunch of powdery snow beneath a size-15 pair of boots.

"Ladies and gentlemen, Betty has left the building," I said under my breath.

I guess if I'd known what was going to happen next, I would have listened to her.

2
THE PHONES

ily, Kelly and Brian are wonderful kids, but you wouldn't want to be around them after they've had sugared cereal. I usually try to get out of the house before the Honeycomb kicks in.

Lily is almost thirteen and learns more in the eighth grade than I did in college. She's cute, but she's also a teenager now and that scares me. Kelly is eleven and wants a horse. She tells me all her friends at school have horses, but I'm not convinced, particularly regarding her friends who live in Hartville Garden Apartments.

"Where do they keep them?" I say.

"Near the tennis courts?" she smiles.

Both are really good with Brian, age seven, and they give Evelyn and me a break every now and then.

My wife, Evelyn, is four years my senior and is sometimes mistaken for my daughter. She looks like she's twenty, exercises, gets lots of rest and at breakfast eats a mixture of puffed wheat and Sandpaper Bran. At least that's what it looks like. She can't stand that I buy the kids the sweet stuff, but it makes them happy, and I feel I do that all too seldom.

As I walk out the door I sometimes hear them say, "Can't Daddy pour our cereal?" If I'm out of the house by 7:30 I avoid the onslaught. I try for quality time, but breakfast isn't quality.

That morning, however, the morning of the column's appearance, I awoke to a strange ringing sensation. It seemed I was floating above myself with a sweet jangling of festive bells, the turkey smell still hanging heavy in the air.

Some people say they dream in color, with every hue and tone in perfect symmetry. They speak of recurring scenes of falling off cliffs or walking on clouds. But I dream in sentences, sometimes complete, sometimes fragments, and I wake with commas and apostrophes floating through my mind. My life is words, and words never sleep. They wait for me, like an old dog curled on the throw rug, tail beating. Words wait and wake me, and spend nights near my lips until they can work their way through my fingers onto a page.

I finally pried my eyes open to see 6:15 on the alarm. A word came to me I will not let escape here. Bad word. Then I heard the sound again—not the bells of St. Mary's as I had originally thought, but the telephone.

Terrible things happen when people call you at 6:15 a.m. You're late for something, or it's a death in the family, or it might be D. J. Starr, which is ten times worse.

"Hello," I said, giving it my best shot to sound awake. I don't know why I try to impress people by trying not to sound like I've just awakened, but I do.

"Jackson Grim, this is D. J. Starr at Hartville Radio and you're on the air!"

In my opinion, morning radio is the gasoline that fuels pop

culture. It is dumbing down via the ionosphere. Cultural pollution transmitted unseen to car stereos, headsets and clock radios. Driven by insipid music, screaming commercials and obnoxious hosts who love to air their disagreements with management, morning radio is the equivalent of an audio Twinkie. It is art laced with MSG with a side of fries, hush puppies and heavily salted opinion. Listeners are dragged through every Hollywood scandal, lurid stories about political leaders and a cacophony of callers who start each sentence with "I just love your show."

Every morning program has someone named Buck, D. J. or Starr. Hartville has two out of three in one person. His real name is Carlin Hardwell. He has worked for sixteen stations in the last fifteen years. They are broadcasting giants in places like Mammoth, Colorado; Pittsfield, Iowa; Tarmac, Minnesota; and Platteville, Wisconsin. D. J.'s frequent live calls to unsuspecting victims are illegal. The lawyers keep telling him that, but he keeps it up because "it's good radio."

D. J. can best be described by the word *annoying*. His voice is annoying. His jokes are annoying. The music he plays is annoying. But just about everybody listens to him at some point in the morning, particularly kids who want to hear the school lunch menu or if there's a closing because of a big snow. For a print guy it's enough to make what little hair I have left stand on end.

D. J.'s shelf life is about eight months to a year in most towns, since it takes about that much time to go through his sound-effects carts and spoof songs. He had been in Hartville about six months when I got the call.

"Hello, D. J.," I said in a fog. "What can I do for you?"

"Well, I hope we're not waking you up, but we just had to comment on your column about the song."

I was surprised he'd finished the comics that early.

"Well, it kind of speaks for itself," I said.

"Now, was this an actual letter delivered to you, or did you come up with it and attribute it to a reader?"

"It was an actual letter, D. J."

A tinny squeak was coming from the phone, because D. J. turns his headphones to an eardrum-splitting level that no one on the planet can stand other than morning show hosts. Radio people naturally like everything loud, particularly when it's their own voice. When D. J. talks off the air he speaks like he's listening to a CD on maximum level, but there is no volume control for him.

D. J. read the poem, and I tried to get out as gracefully as I could. I thanked him for mentioning the story and encouraged people to pick up an extra copy of the paper for family members. I figured Betty would appreciate the plug. I tried to humor him and profusely thanked him for the call, but before I could get off the phone D. J. interrupted me.

"Go ahead, caller," D. J. said.

"Hello? Am I on?"

"Yes, go ahead!"

"My name is Harold Whinnel, from over on Pine Bluff, and if the words to that song weren't so true I'd be laughing right along with you."

"What do you mean, Harold? You pretty upset about the city council, huh?" D. J. said.

"You bet I am—I mean, I don't bet—I mean, yessir I'm upset. The first thing they do is put an *X* for Christmas and then they take away our manger. Next they'll be coming for our churches, telling us we can't read the Bible."

"I don't think that's what the council . . ." I said, coming out of the fog, but D. J. cut me off again.

"Well, it looks like a lot of you have opinions on this one, because the phone lines are jammed."

There is an axiom in radio that a person's voice *never* matches a person's looks. Most people had never seen D. J. or the inner workings of the station. When he said, "The phone lines are jammed," listeners thought of a control board with a maze of buttons and flashing lights that would scare an air-traffic controller. In their minds D. J. was about thirty-five with short, brown hair, maybe a mustache, 6'2", trim and clean-shaven.

But I had been to the station. I had seen D. J. I knew what was happening. D. J. was just a tad under 5'4" with a goatlike beard he constantly stroked. His face was round like a gnome's, and his fingers were stubby and yellow from nicotine. An overflowing ashtray sat at his side, and wire copy was piled on the turntables beside him. The station still hadn't sprung for a CD player and just barely had enough money to keep the tape machine heads cleaned.

The "jammed phone lines" were exactly two lights that blinked haphazardly by D. J.'s side. There was only one on-air phone line hooked into the control board, so to get response from callers other than the guest D. J. hit the speakerphone in front of him and grabbed a coat hanger suspended from the ceiling. At the end of the hanger, gray electrical tape secured a dented Electro-voice microphone. In my mind I could see him bend the hanger with a jerk, ashes scattering. I heard his headphones squeal again as he pushed the button for another call.

"Yeah, what do you think?"

"Am I on?"

"Yeah, this is Hartville Radio, go ahead."

Larry King had nothing to worry about.

"This all started when they took prayer and the Ten Commandments out of the schools."

"How's that?" D. J. said.

"Well, this is the effect. We can't even celebrate Christmas without worrying about being politically correct. Jesus is the reason for the season. It's as simple as that."

I tried to respond, but D. J. was having too much fun egging the callers on. He hung up and immediately punched in another, who pointed blame a little closer to home.

"The guy you have on there right now is part of the problem, D. J. He's part of the media elite that wants to set their agenda, and if it wasn't for programs like yours, we probably wouldn't hear a thing about what's going on at City Hall."

I don't think I'm part of the media elite. I worked my way through Hartville College and eked out a journalism degree. After an internship at the paper I started beat reporting and finally graduated to the column. I basically do that and whatever else Betty assigns to me. Don't get me wrong. I'm not saying I'm a conservative, but Dan Rather and I don't do lunch every month to plot our next stack of biased stories. It just doesn't happen.

I tried to explain, but D. J. just kept taking more calls. It was like throwing lighter fluid into a fireplace. The flames grew hotter, the voices licked higher on the air, and I was getting sick. It was morning radio at its best, or worst, depending on your point of view.

The conservatives in Hartville had been quiet, almost subdued, in their reaction to the council's decision. The evil in the culture was so great, it seemed they were resigned to watch passively. But the column sparked something. Like a rushing underground current, the Christians suddenly rose to the surface and took the rest of Hartville with them.

That afternoon the phone rang. And rang. And rang. Betty swished by and gave me the "I told you so" look, though she never actually said it.

Mostly the callers were fundamentalists upset about the direction of the country and particularly the way the City Council and the media were X-ing Christ out of Christmas. I responded by saying I was the one who had printed the letter; if I was biased, why would I have let it go through? The logic didn't work. Most felt it was a fluke, that a story had gotten by the gatekeeper, which it had.

It was curious to me that the religious community was angry with the culture they had retreated from so many years earlier. They had constructed their own Christian ghetto inside America with Christian bookstores, Christian radio stations, Christian workout videos, Christian recording artists, Christian comedians, Christian T-shirts, Christian antioxidants and Christian aluminum siding complete with fish symbols.

Around two o'clock my ear was red and stinging from all the calls. I picked up the phone on the first ring and said, "I know you're angry about the culture and Jesus is the reason for the season. Okay?"

"Mr. Grim?"

"Yes."

"This is Pastor Marty Karlsen at Hartville Community Church, and I just want to thank you for printing the letter this morning."

"You do?"

"Yes, I think you've done a great service to the Christian community in this town. There are some of us who are too lily-livered to take a stand for the faith, and you've helped galvanize us."

Karlsen talked with a slight drawl, like he was a transplant from the South, which was weird because he was actually Swedish. I imagined him putting barbecue sauce on his lutefisk. His voice was low and gravelly, with a tremolo that bleated occasionally, somewhat like Mr. Haney on *Green Acres*. I assumed he was probably good at what he did, stirring people up and reassuring them that they were on the path to heaven, though religion isn't my thing.

"I did all that?" I said.

"We won't know the entire effect until the school board meeting next week, but I'd say your writing, though you haven't always been a friend of our cause, has helped a great deal. That's unusual because of the liberal bias I know you have, but still there's reason to rejoice."

"What's supposed to happen at the school board meeting?" I said, intentionally ignoring the bias comment.

"Our public schools have abandoned the historic Judeo-Christian tradition. Secular humanists have taken over, and the multiculturalists of the day have changed the curriculum from reading, writing and arithmetic to classes in womyn's studies and whole language and outcome-based education and inventive spelling . . ."

I checked out just after the secular humanism quote and put it on autopilot, because I had heard the same thing all morning and even at lunch. All I wanted was a ham sandwich from the deli, but I couldn't get to the counter without someone stepping in front and saying, "You're that column guy, aren't you?" These people were everywhere.

"So during the school board meeting," Marty said as I checked back in, "a group of concerned citizens will give their views about the content of the new Winter Celebration at the school. We're praying it's going to be a victory for all Bible-believing Christians in Hartville and hopefully throughout the United States!"

I let my answering machine pick up the calls for an hour or

so while I composed my column for the next day. It wasn't hard to choose a topic. I took excerpts from conversations, most of them angry at media attitudes toward Christians and the truth of the song I had printed.

I received one call from Dierdra Bergman Freep, who said she was appalled that I would "turn to religion to sell papers."

"These crazy, wacko fundamentalists think God gave them the right to run everybody's life. They want to elect a preacher as president and run the country from their churches."

The previous year Dierdra's group, Atheists Against Mangers, had singlehandedly wrenched the manger from the lawn of City Hall. A.A.M. was small, but when you use a lawyer's stationery to correspond with the city, people pay attention. When the council discovered a legal precedent called the "reindeer rule," Jesus returned, sharing the space with Frosty and Rudolph.

"These people need to get over their love affair with the manger," Dierdra had said. "They're followers, like sheep, mostly lower-class, uneducated and easy to lead. Religion is in their DNA."

The town had gone into a general state of shock after that statement. Many of the religious folk had protested, but most just shook their heads and figured they couldn't do anything to stop her.

So I finished the article while listening to my answering machine click and beep and wheeze. It finally sputtered and gave up the tape. It was sad watching it spin its final bit of oxide across the playhead, but I guess we're all appointed a certain number of days on this earth. I wasn't sure how people would react to the second column, but I felt it was the least I could do in tribute to the fallen machine.

The next day I found out D. J. had done his homework. After

my call on the morning show, he had challenged others in town to come up with their own songs and audition to sing them on the air.

Being sensitive to the townsfolk, I would describe Hartville as musically challenged. We have no center for performing arts. There is no Hartville orchestra. The Barbershop Quartet Society left town because they couldn't find four people who could sing in the same key.

But with all those strikes against them, the people of Hartville rose to the occasion. I guess hell hath no fury like an angry Christian with a guitar.

Betty taped the whole program the next morning and gave it to me on two cassettes. Here's a portion of the transcript of the songs from the broadcast.

D. J.:	All right, our first presentation will be some gentlemen from—where was it again?
BASS VOICE:	Hartville Community Church. We're the men's quartet.
D. J.:	And all three of you are a part of that?
TENOR VOICE:	Yes sir.
D. J.:	Where's the fourth guy?
BASS VOICE:	We don't have a fourth guy.
D. J.:	Then how can you be a quartet?
BASS VOICE:	The church already had a men's trio.
D. J.:	I see. So the quartet is going to sing what?
BASS VOICE:	This is our version of "Good Christian Men, Rejoice."
D. J.:	And what is that one about?
BASS VOICE:	The original was a song proclaiming the good news that Jesus was born, but this version is called "Good Secular Men, Rejoice."

D. J.:   Well, [squeal] I'm sure we'll all catch on. Get up
                    to the microphone there so we can all hear you.
(There are muffled sounds of rattling paper and general con-
fusion of the quartet until the discordant strum of a guitar is
heard, along with the a cappella harmony of three men lumber-
ing around the melody.)

Good secular men, rejoice
With heart and soul and voice.
Give ye heed to what we say: News! News!
Don't sing your Christmas song today.
Sing of reindeers and of Claus,
Just don't say "Jesus" now because
We'll be sued today, we'll be sued today.

Good liberal men, with zest
Hire lawyers to protest.
File briefs aplenty and with flair: Bill! Bill!
Christ isn't for the public square.
Play tunes by Springsteen and John Tesh,
Tear down our dear old Christmas crèche,
File a suit today, file a suit today.

Good libbers, we won't leave you out.
We don't want you to scream and shout.
Religion is for all those men: Pigs! Pigs!
Who oppress the good womyn.
You want equal time to pray
To god your Mother? This we say,
"You are not correct, you are not correct."

Revisionists, this is our last verse.
No need to clamor or to curse.
The Bible it is full of flaws: Revise! Revise!
Strike out the miracles because
They can't be true; you want to pray
To the Eternal It today?
Thanks, but no thanks; thanks, but no thanks.

D. J.:	Hey, I've heard that one before, and you guys are pretty good, huh?
FEMALE VOICE:	[applause and giggles] Really good, D. J.
BASS VOICE:	And we'd like to invite everybody to the church this Sunday . . .
D. J.:	Yeah, yeah, that's great. Now we've got somebody else here—thank you, boys.
FEMALE VOICE:	Hi, D. J.
D. J.:	Any you must be Jenny Logan, right?
JENNY:	That's right, I'm home-schooled with my three brothers and sisters, and we're learning a lot about the history of Christmas hymns this year.
D. J.:	Okay, and what are you going to sing?
JENNY:	We chose one of people's favorite Christmas songs, "Silent Night."
D. J.:	Yeah, I think everybody likes that one.
JENNY:	But in this version, it's kind of like a parody, you know? Well, I sing a song Franz Gruber never thought of. He was the German guy who didn't know any better and put in all those politically incorrect words like *holy*, *Savior* and *heaven*. I've come up with a version that won't offend so many people as kind of a commentary on mod-

	ern society.
D. J.:	And how old are you?
JENNY:	Twelve.
D. J.:	Wow! When I was twelve I couldn't even pronounce half the words you just used. Is that a cassette player you have there?
JENNY:	Yes, my mom played the organ at church, and we recorded it. And just so you know, my mom wrote the last verse especially for our family.
D. J.:	All right, ladies and jellyfish, here she is, the beautiful Jenny Logan with her "Silent Night," the P.C. version.

Silent night, Solstice night,
All is calm, all half price.
Round yon department store, all of us strangers,
Wondering who will get the last Power Rangers,
Shop in heavenly peace, shop in heavenly peace.

Silent night, wonderful night,
All the house filled with light.
Round the windows, shrubs and flowerpots,
Blinking lights, burning thousands of watts:
Sleep with blindfolds on, sleep with blindfolds on.

Silent night, Christmas night,
All the toys out of sight.
Dad in his nightshirt and me with my caps
Trudge up to bed, and then we collapse.
There has got to be more. Surely there's something more.

Another highlight of the broadcast was an a cappella version of "Away With the Manger" sung by D. J. himself.

I thought the whole thing might die down with everybody making fun of the situation. But it didn't. Things got worse.

3

RUDOLPH THE NOSELESS REINDEER

anta has never been a militant figure to me. He's always been kind of cute and cuddly with the presents, round belly and reindeer. But to the religious right in town, he's the worst. Switch a couple of letters around in his name and you get Satan. He's that bad.

Santa made his incarnations at several retailers in town. Mostly he was ringing bells outside the grocery and department stores. But the St. Nicks of Hartville appeared to have eating disorders. They were thin, with beards that hung in clumps, and they wore badly faded red suits and black coverings over tennis shoes that no one but true believers thought were boots.

It was the first Monday in December, and the school board meeting was two days away. You could feel the tension in the air.

People were still talking about D. J.'s program and my column. In a small town you tend to cling to such things.

The anti-Christmas contingent was on the sideline, gloating over all the furor. They had won in the courts. The law was on their side. And they had Dierdra Bergman Freep as their spokesperson, which created a sense of resolve and contentment in the ranks.

But the Christians were slowly organizing their troops. Pastor Karlsen was busy recording his daily fifteen-minute radio program for the local Christian station. The original name of the program had been *The Freedom Hour.* When they realized the incongruity of the program's title and length, though, they changed it to *Heart to Hartville.* The station really didn't have an opinion since it would be paid no matter what the name, so they aired it every day at 10:00 a.m., right after the farm report.

The format of the program consisted of the announcer, Deacon Immer Wright, talking over an ancient recording of Squire Parson's "Beulah Land." Deacon Wright owned Wright's Hardware, the current site of the Christmas crèche. He had it displayed on the sidewalk in front of his store, and when anyone of like mind passed, they honked and the deacon would appear inside the window in front of the "Jesus Is the Reason for the Season" banner. Deacon Wright did not have an announcer's voice, but like D. J. he loved to hear it, whether it was during a prayer meeting or on the radio. And since he underwrote half the cost of the show's airtime, he'd made the strong suggestion that he introduce the pastor at the start of each program. No one on the church board objected.

Deacon Wright always ended his introduction with "And now, from our heart to yours, here's the pastor of Hartville Community Church, Marty Karlsen."

With "Beulah Land" swelling in the background, Pastor Karlsen would begin his Bible study. When he was finished, Deacon Wright would return with announcements and the closing theme, more "Beulah Land."

On this Monday, Karlsen introduced a series of programs he called "Turning Back the Night" to mobilize stealth Christians who would denounce the secularization of the Christmas holiday. The program was so special that they had decided to change the theme of the show to "Onward Christian Soldiers." This put pressure on the deacon: it was live, it was different, and it confused him to no end. It had taken months for him to memorize his opening lines.

The broadcast began with music, then the deacon said, "Welcome to *Heart to Hartville,* a daily broadcast of inspiration and encouragement that . . . uh . . . helps you turn back the night . . ."

"Onward Christian soldiers, marching as to war . . ."

"And now, from the heart . . . of . . . ours to yours, here's Pastor Karlsen. [barely audible] I told you we should have recorded it, Marty."

Karlsen commended those who took their faith seriously and urged listeners to "exercise their God-given right to speak out against the darkness." He was referring to the Wednesday-night school board meeting, of course, but as he spoke an idea began forming in the brain of Deacon Wright. When the pastor finished two minutes early, concluding with "They have perverted everything they've put their slimy hands on. We need to put the devil in his place and the secular humanists with him," the door was open for a move of the Spirit.

"I feel in my heart," Deacon Wright said, "that we ought to seize this opportunity to really show these people we mean business."

The recording room was situated behind the main studio of the radio station, with nothing between but double-paned glass. The operator on duty later told me he glanced back just as the deacon began his speech and saw Marty Karlsen's eyes "wide as the south end of a northbound elephant."

"I have some posters and wood at the hardware store that I'd like to donate to anyone who will put their feet where their mouth is and walk around City Hall to show we mean what we say."

If you listen closely to the tape, you'll hear Pastor Karlsen clear his throat repeatedly, increasingly closer to the microphone.

"And I say this afternoon is the perfect time to put your faith into action. [Ahem] We need creative people who can print placards and think up catchy sayings and more people to walk around City Hall. [AHEM]"

". . . With the cross of Jesus, going on before."

*　*　*

The city building, just a block from Hartville's main shopping area, is arguably the prettiest structure in the county. It was built fifty years ago with huge stones from a nearby quarry, so it is marked by a stateliness, elegance and charm that will continue long after this generation leaves the planet.

The lawn in front of City Hall sports several oaks; two huge cedars are positioned strategically at the entrance. In November and December the lights on the trees reflect from the glass in the hall, giving a double illumination effect. When there is a light coating of snow on the ground, you'll often see children playing on the undulating lawn. Families pose for holiday newsletter pictures.

To the dismay of Christians, City Hall's dignity is marred by an ungainly appendage between Thanksgiving and Christmas each year. A red trailer is chained to a parking meter on the east side of City Hall. A sign hanging slightly askew says "Santa's Workshop." Children are brought into the dimly lit room, most of them wailing and kicking, and have their picture taken with another bony Santa. This of course is an exercise for the parents, not the children, and Santa does a brisk business in Hartville.

A small gray speaker mounted on top of the trailer plays a tinny "Rudolph" by Gene Autry and the Peanuts theme by Vince Guaraldi. Every thirty seconds Mrs. Santa invites the "kiddies" waiting outside to think hard about what they want her husband to bring them this year. On this fateful night Mrs. Santa was in rare form.

Not far away, about fifty people huddled together in front of City Hall with signs that read "Jesus Is the Reason for the Season," "Put Christ Back in Christmas" and "Santa Didn't Die for Your Sins!" The sun was nearly finished for the day, and shoppers scurried along with their bags. A line about fifteen deep formed in front of Santa's place as parents tried to beat closing time.

Deacon Wright, a former marine, and looking somewhat like Bull Conner at a civil rights march, led the way, encouraging his followers by chanting, "You can't take our holiday!"

They repeated in unison, "You can't take our holiday!"

"It's in our heart and here to stay!"

"Sound off, Jesus!"

"Sound off, he's born!"

There are conflicting reports about how the fight began. Some say one of the elves asked the marchers to lower the volume of their singing. Others contend it was the nasally sound of Gene Autry that pushed the protesters over the brink. Whatever it was, the next day the headline on the front of the *Daily News* said, "Police Arrest Four in Skirmish with Santa."

Christmas is supposed to bring peace on earth, goodwill to men, but just the opposite happened at City Hall last night.

Four protesters were arrested, then released after allegedly attacking Santa Claus at his holiday workshop. One elf was also slightly injured.

About 50 people holding banners and singing Christmas songs criticized the recent decision concerning the presence of a manger scene on government property. The fight broke out shortly after 5:30 p.m.

"We were just minding our own business, taking pictures with the kids, when those people showed up," said the elf, who requested anonymity. "It was awful. They broke the nose off of Rudolph and nearly killed Santa."

Immer Wright, owner of Wright's Hardware and deacon at Hartville Community Church, was involved in the melee.

"I don't really know what started it," Wright said. "All I know is that we've got the right to protest just as much as they have the right to merchandise a sacred holiday."

A shaken Santa refused to file charges against the group, saying he did not want to reveal his identity. The red-suited man was so upset by the ordeal that he asked the children in line to return Tuesday for complimentary photos and visits.

The incident comes in the wake of public outcry spurred by columnist Jackson Grim, who included a politically correct Christmas Hymn in his column, and it comes two days prior to a school board meeting where citizens are expected to turn out in record numbers.

Marty Karlsen, pastor of Hartville Community Church, where many of the protesters attend, said he was distressed about the outbreak of violence over the issue.

"Many people in our congregation feel very strongly about

celebrating Christmas the right way," Karlsen said. "We certainly don't condone violence, and if I were to talk with Santa, or the man who was playing Santa—of course we all know he wasn't the real . . . I mean, well, if I could speak to whoever it was underneath that fake beard and red suit, I would ask him to reconsider the perpetration of a lie to the children of this community. We would, of course, like to help him repair his reindeer if that can be done.

"That doesn't mean we're pro-Santa," he added. "We're just pro-people, no matter who they dress up as."

When I read the article Tuesday morning, I wondered what Dierdra Bergman Freep was thinking. I figured she would show up at the Wednesday meeting with her sons, Tim and Rob. And I figured this was one school board meeting I couldn't afford to miss.

4

GOD IN THE SNOWBANK

hristmas always brings out the best in people. That's what I've heard, but don't believe it. The truth is, Christmas should bring out the best in people, but it doesn't.

There are always the niceties of fruitcake and gift fudge sent by relatives who have no business making either. There's an occasional smile amidst the scramble for the last overpriced action figure or hot doll of the season.

But most people live in their own world at Christmas, in a hurry and looking for presents that might make them feel they haven't blown it this year. Especially men. Christmas brings to all males a deep need to be satisfied, for love and warmth. A man wants to please his wife and kids, but Christmas expectations hang over him like an overgrown evergreen. The tree that looks so bright and healthy in December eventually drops needles on the carpet which are discovered around March, when he's barefoot and least expecting it.

Christmas is an endless winter of expectations. The child thinks, *I hope I don't get clothes,* while the parent thinks, *She's really going to like the turtleneck and leggings.* The mother ponders all the possibilities. *I just don't want him to put it off and spend too much,* she says to herself, while the husband thinks, *Next year I'm not going to put it off and spend so much, but at least she'll be happy with this rhinestone hair dryer.*

The husband then focuses on himself. After a harrowing evening of traffic, zigzagging through endless hordes of equally clueless husbands, he muses, *Just once, just one Christmas, may it not be a tie. Or a sweater. Or a book that someone else wanted to read—someone who hopes you'll leave it lying around so they can pick it up. Just once let it be something that makes me feel like a child again.*

But Christmas can never make you feel like a child unless you are ready for it. The busyness and the lists and the expectations crowd the day. We fall over ourselves hanging happiness on the eaves and plastering joy on the wall, and still Christmas ends and we wonder what happened. Broken joy can't be replaced like Christmas lights.

This is what Christmas meant to me that year. Between Thanksgiving and the 25th of December, I checked out. I was there when we trimmed the tree and opened the presents, but not all there. Christmases past had taught me to hold back. I laughed at the delight of the kids and their excitement when they tore into the gifts, but deep down it was like watching someone root for the Chicago Cubs or the Boston Red Sox, who never win. You had to feel sorry for the little saps. They just didn't get it.

You can't win at Christmas. You can't ever really have joy because there's something staring you in the face called LIFE, and I don't mean the magazine. Life is there with its hopes and dreams like ornaments on the tree. After years of life, you realize these ornaments aren't real. You pick them off a week after the big day and wrap the dreams in paper. You stuff hope in a dusty box and shove it in a closet until next year, when you're a little older and a little closer to being recycled like the tree in the living room.

Man, Christmas is just downright depressing!

It helped that I was in the middle of the hullabaloo about the "Away With the Manger" column. People in town who had never noticed me before came up and patted me on the back and said, "Hey, Jackson, hey, you're the one that wrote that column, aren't you?" And I would say, "Yes I am," and they would smile and say, "Hey, that column was something else." And then they would laugh or just stare at me as if they could look into my eyes and see another column growing somewhere between my cornea and brain. Or they would scuff at the ground with one foot and grin uncomfortably, not knowing what to do. So I'd say I needed to go to the grocery to pick up a cantaloupe and that usually got me out of there.

But underneath all the activity was an emptiness and a sense that I was in big trouble. *We* were in big trouble. The whole town was sitting on a powder keg, antsy for something to happen, and it affected everyone's mental state.

Again, it showed up on the air.

Calls were coming in to the program *Your Turn* on Hartville Radio. A snowdrift closed down one of the main roads, and, as happens in small towns, weather became news. It was as if we'd never seen snow before. *Your Turn*'s host, Darby Gardner, at some point in his life had taught sociology at a junior college. We picked that up because he would mention it about every five minutes. He now sold insurance and gave advice on mutual funds that he just happened to sell at a pretty good commission, but the love of his life was *Your Turn*. It was his gift to Hartville.

"It's *Your Turn*, with Darby Gardner," the announcer would say, quickly followed by swelling music that reminded me of the *Captain Kangaroo* theme. "Now, heeeeeeeere's Darby."

On the news prior to the show the road closing was the top story, closely followed by the school board meeting, with a veiled reference to my column. When Darby gave his introduction for the evening's topic, he said it had taken him twice as long as usual to get to the studio because of the snowdrift. Then he added that the wind had blown the snow into such a strange shape that it took on a ghostly effect and he couldn't get it out of his mind.

The school board meeting led Darby's list of gripes. It had been the main topic for the past three nights, but a caller jumped on the snowdrift reference immediately. The voice was a bit quavery, and I imagined a rotary dial, a wrinkled face and skin underneath her arms hanging like the wattle of a turkey.

CALLER 1:   Darby, I saw the same thing on the news, and I was wondering if anyone else noticed it. I'm glad you mentioned it.

DARBY: And what was it you saw?

CALLER 1:   It looked like an angel to me. The angel Gabriel maybe. You could see its wings up by the interstate overpass and then down at the bottom the face. Did you see that?

DARBY: Well, no, I can't say that I perceived anything angelic about it, but let's find out if anyone agrees with you. Hello?

CALLER 2:   Yeah, I saw it, only I didn't see no angel.

DARBY: You were driving there?

CALLER 2:   I went by it on the way to the store. Now I'm not a religious nut, and I haven't been into this

	manger thing that much, but it looked to me like those pictures of Jesus we used to take home from Sunday school when we were kids. I could see the beard and the long hair and everything.
DARBY:	Very interesting—so there seems to be a religious element to the sightings so far. Thank you. Yes, you're on the air.
CALLER 3:	Yeah, hi, Darby. I seen it on the news and it looked to me like it was a possum in the middle with its tail wrapped around a limb, then over in the right corner there was a militarylike person hunched over and eating a can of Spam.
DARBY:	Well, that's a new one. I can't say I saw that. Let's take another and see if anyone else thinks they see something.
CALLER 4:	Love your show, Darby.
DARBY:	Thank you.
CALLER 4:	I think it looks like, and I'm not saying it was actually him, but I think it looks like Uncle Jed from the *Beverly Hillbillies*.
DARBY:	Interesting that you would use the name of the character on that program instead of Buddy Ebsen. There was a study not too long ago that looked at the sociological significance of the media's influence on culture. I used to teach a class that dealt with some of those issues and . . .
CALLER 4:	Well, I don't know about that, but it looked like Uncle Jed to me. That's all I'm saying.
DARBY:	All right, yes, one more then.
CALLER 5:	I saw the one that lady was talking about.
DARBY:	Buddy Ebsen?

CALLER 5:   No, the one that looked like Jesus in the take-
               home papers. I think with all that's going on in
               this town, we're getting a sign from God!

This went on for quite some time, with people seeing everything in the snow from the Holy Grail to General Custer. But
overwhelmingly people said they saw Jesus, the manger, the wise
men or a member of the Holy Family.

They were still talking the next night when half the town met
in the school gymnasium, and for many the image had changed
in the interim. The person who had said she saw the possum
called D. J. in the morning and swore it now looked like Elvis
Presley in Blue Hawaii. I suspected Betty, of course. I sat near the
front right, behind Dierdra Bergman Freep and her contingent
from Atheists Against Mangers.

No matter what you think of her, Dierdra is an interesting
character. I had written a feature story about her when she first
reared her atheistic head in public. She seemed to like the publicity, though she looked with suspicion at the questions I asked.
When I tried to find out more about her personal side, she refused to answer, and I had to rely on secondary sources who lived
in her old hometown. I didn't put those findings in the story, but
much of it made sense.

Dierdra had not always been antagonistic to religion. In fact,
she was raised attending church, but an abusive father and teen-
age rebellion sent her away—at least that's what the sources said.
The final straw came when Dierdra's husband, who was heavily
involved in a church, abandoned her after Rob was born, leaving
her with nothing but a mortgage and two fatherless boys. That
was when she went back to her maiden name and took on a look
that would frighten a defensive lineman. I suspect most people
in Hartville who hated Dierdra for her stand would have been

kinder had they known her situation.

Behind me several churchgoers commented on the broadcast and made references to "those people," who sat only a couple of rows away. A journalist/columnist always likes to be in the middle of a story, but I'll admit it seemed a little too close for comfort.

The school board, accustomed to a small room with no audience, timidly made its way to the long table with a microphone at each seat. Cameras from the local television station were there, and several members shielded their eyes from the harsh lights as they were seated. They looked like sacrificial lambs heading for the altar.

When Jeannette Harris, head of the board, asked us to stand for the Pledge of Allegiance, I heard Dierdra say, "Here we go." The following is my earwitness account.

"I pledge allegiance to the flag [cough] the United States of America. [Louder cough] And to the republic, for which it stands. [Several coughs] One nation, under [A COUGH CRESCENDO], indivisible, with liberty and justice for all."

Both of Dierdra's sons were with her that evening. Tim was eight and in the third grade. Already his shoulders sagged from two years of teasing and derision from other kids. You can imagine what a last name like Freep will do to a child. On top of that, the leading atheist in town was his mother. The word that comes to mind when I think of Tim is *reluctant.* His life was like a video game with no controls. He could only sit and watch.

His brother, Rob, was four and had not yet been exposed to the cruelty of others. He sat quietly for the first few minutes, then got out of his chair and ran around the gymnasium the rest of the night. I think one of the TV people gave him a lens cap to play with so he wouldn't trip over their cables, and he used it as a Frisbee throughout the proceedings.

Jeannette Harris took control of the meeting and explained that they would give as many as possible a chance to voice their opinion. The subject was the school's annual "Winter Celebration," and they would take comments from parents immediately after the old business.

The old business had gone nearly forty-five minutes when Dierdra stood up and yelled, "You can stop stalling and get to it, because I'm not going home until I have my say."

This brought a general round of applause from the crowd, and I believe it may have been the first time the two sides had agreed on anything. Jeannette closed one book and opened another on the table. Carl Luntgren, a toadish-looking man with little hair and much girth, motioned for new business, and immediately people lined up behind the single microphone in the center aisle, just behind the free-throw line. A lens cap sailed by my head. Rob followed not far behind.

A young woman of about thirty was the first to speak. She had blond hair and wore a loose-fitting blouse and jeans that said she was practical rather than fashion-conscious. She had a rich alto voice that reverberated to the back of the gym and forward again.

"My name is Cheryl Fortney, and I have three children who attend Hartville Elementary. When I was a child I walked these same halls and even had some of the same teachers my children have."

She was reading from note cards stacked in her hand. Soon, however, she pushed them together and held them behind her back.

"I'm a Christian," she said determinedly. "And Christmas is a very special holiday for me and my family. I think the majority of people feel this way in our community. And for you to strike out the very meaning of Christmas from the songs and activities of our children is just plain wrong.

"Two of my children are in the musical this year, and when they showed me what they were allowed to sing, it just broke my heart. There was no 'Joy to the World,' no 'Hark the Herald Angels Sing.' There was Frosty and Rudolph and 'Here Comes Santa Claus,' but no mention of the reason we celebrate.

"I understand there are people in this community who don't believe in Jesus. Well, I don't believe in Santa or Rudolph, but I don't bar those songs. Why can't we have traditional Christmas carols included? What are we so afraid of?"

"If you'll recall," Carl Luntgren said, shifting in his folding chair, "the kids are singing 'Silent Night,' and last I heard that was a Christmas song."

Dierdra applauded, and her group followed along after she gave them a stern look.

"But they aren't allowed to sing it," Cheryl said. "They were told they had to hum it along with the instruments while one child read about the meaning of Kwanzaa."

Murmurs of disdain filtered through the audience. Carl shifted again, the chair squeaking painfully as if the rivets were about to pop.

"We appreciate your opinion," Jeannette said. "May we have the next, please?"

A tall, thin man stepped to the microphone and leaned down. He tapped it with his finger, then blew into it. His work clothes were soiled and hung on him like sheets on a clothesline. There was a halting drawl to his voice, and he chewed his words like tobacco.

"I'm Randy Cline. I live just over on Sycamore, and we've got two kids who go here. I don't understand how we can justify taking God out of the schools and putting in clinics that give out

. . . well, that give out things we wouldn't even think of talking about a few years ago. You've taken down the Ten Commandments. You've said our kids can't pray in school. In one school they put a bag over a picture of Jesus until the Supreme Court said they had to take the whole thing down. And now you're taking Christmas away from us. That ain't right."

Most of the crowd roared in approval and applauded until Jeannette Harris banged the table and called for order.

"I just don't understand what we're coming to," Randy continued. "Our money says 'In God We Trust'; our pledge says 'one nation under God,' if you could hear it over the coughs tonight. We were founded as a Christian nation. And if you want to clean up the violence and gangs and all the problems we have, you ought not kick God out of the classroom but welcome him back in. That's all I have to say."

There was more applause as Randy stepped out of the way. He slid back into the sea of faces as Dierdra Bergman Freep grabbed the microphone and pushed the others out of the way.

"Right here is the problem the board has already addressed and addressed correctly," Dierdra said. "These fundamentalist Christians want everything their way, and when they don't get their way they try to impose their values on the rest of us. This school is for my boys. This school is for all the children of Hartville, not just Christians. There are Jews and Muslims and atheists and all kinds of people represented here, and the courts of our land have spoken. The government should not endorse a religion."

The applause was replaced by a low boo and a few hisses, but Dierdra's voice cut through the noise.

"Christianity has been responsible for more persecution and atrocities over the centuries than any other belief system. They believe in a virgin birth and a three-headed God and other wacky things that I don't even want my children exposed to, let alone made to believe. If they want to check out intellectually from this society and go to some hillside and live in caves, that's fine with me. But speaking for our society and others who are concerned about true freedom, a public school is no place to be advancing religion, so I would ask that if you have to have a program, you keep the Winter Celebration the way it is."

Another chorus of boos filled the room as Dierdra passed the gauntlet of jeering parents. She fed off their hatred. Her steps became more resolute, and by the time she got back to her chair she was smiling and laughing.

"Put that in your column, Grim," she said to me.

Another highlight of the meeting occurred when a short, well-dressed man came in through the side door. He wore designer gloves, a designer trench coat and designer shoes. The man at the microphone seemed to recognize him and stepped aside in favor of the new arrival. His gait was every bit as determined as Dierdra's, and we all knew he was a lawyer from the moment he banged on the outside door that said "No Entrance." He seemed like the type of man who would tell you how many times he had been before the Supreme Court and would do just about anything to get back there.

"My name is Hewitt Lawrence III, from Lawrence, Packer and Davidovic in Washington, D.C."

He spoke with every inch of his body, rising on his toes when he said important words and making eye contact with each board member.

"We are very concerned about what's going on in this school, and we are pursuing legal action in accordance with the statutes of state and federal law as it pertains to the Winter Celebration being performed here at . . ." He checked his notes. "Excuse me, um—Hartville? Is that where I am? Oh yes, here it is. Hartville Elementary.

"We are also serving you and the city with legal notices regarding this infringement of rights by our clients, which I would say is the view represented by the majority of those in attendance tonight [APPLAUSE], so that we have the opportunity for free speech rights in our songs, in the erection of a crèche on public property and to have open discourse in the public square."

Hewitt Lawrence III pulled a letter from his pocket and held it in his hand. It was only a business-sized envelope, but he wielded it like a machete.

"For too long people of faith have been silent about their rights, and I am here to say those days are over. I've argued thirteen cases before the Supreme Court, and our firm has filed countless friend-of-the-court briefs in cases that concern religious liberty. I want the people of Hartville to know that I will personally fight this all the way to those hallowed chambers again if I have to, but I would plead with the school board tonight, and I'll put it before the City Council as well: Stop barring the good people of this town from exercising what the Constitution freely gives.

" 'Congress shall make no law respecting an establishment of religion or prohibiting the free exercise thereof.' That's what's at stake here. The framers of that document, Jefferson and Madison particularly, wrote about a wall of separation between church and state. But the wall exists not to protect the government from people who want to talk about Jesus, but to protect the church from the greedy fingers of federal rulers."

The applause crescendoed, and Hewitt Lawrence III had the good sense to end his speech on an up note. He handed the letter to Jeannette Harris, who held it like a biology-lab frog; then he quickly left the building through the "No Exit" door.

The meeting lasted till nearly 1:00 a.m., but I went back to the office at 8:30 to get my column in for the morning's final edition. I don't know whether it was the writing, the subject matter or the personalities involved, but my view of the meeting ran in several papers in the county and was picked up nationally in the "What Other Papers Are Saying" column.

That was where a New York producer saw the piece and set up what would become the most memorable media event in town history.

5
PHYLLIS
COMES
TO HARTVILLE

f radio made the people of Hartville sound like idiots, television showed it in living color.

On Friday of the same week, Pastor Marty Karlsen was in his study preparing "Turning Back the Night" scripts for *Heart to Hartville*. Mildred, his long-time secretary, who prided herself on her ability to keep her pastor interruption-free, reluctantly handed him a call slip that said "Tony Rockonsini, New York." He wasn't surprised to find out the name had been badly misspelled, but he was jolted when he heard a female voice on the line.

"Teauni," as he discovered, was calling from one of about a thousand talk shows based in New York. The host, "Phyllis," wanted to come to Hartville and hold a town meeting of sorts. All the major players would be part of the story: Atheists Against

Mangers, school board officials, a representative from City Hall and a strong contingent of the Christian community, headed by none other than the Reverend Karlsen.

"How do I know you're going to be fair?" Karlsen said. "How do I know you're not going to come down here and make fools of us and cut us off in the middle of our sentences?"

"I can assure you Phyllis would never permit that," Teauni said reassuringly. She seemed so nice and genuine and understanding. "Phyllis is a very religious person herself and wants to let you tell your story as a microcosm of all the conflict there is in society about freedom of speech and religious issues."

Teauni was quite compelling, quite persuasive. By the time Karlsen hung up, he felt Phyllis was doing the congregation a great favor by allowing it to host her nationwide broadcast in Hartville Community Church. Besides, the pastor believed it was time "for the Lord to have his say in these matters."

As it turned out, Karlsen had no reason to gloat about being the first one contacted by Teauni. Simultaneously other producers and assistant producers and assistants to the assistant producers were calling every possible contact in Hartville, filling out personality sheets and rating from 1 to 5 such things as "strength of voice," "communicates well" and "grasps issues."

By the time the calls were made, just about everyone in Hartville believed they were going to be the priority guest for the broadcast. The mayor called his wife. Deacon Wright called a special staff prayer meeting at the hardware store. Dierdra Bergman Freep made a hair appointment, and D. J. Starr bought a tie. He had a total of three in his closet, but he decided he wanted something that didn't clip on.

The whole town buzzed for the next few days as satellite trucks and network syndication representatives arrived. For once the

Blue Star Motel was full. Immediately following the Sunday-morning service, a technical crew started setup in the sanctuary for the Monday broadcast. The church canceled its Sunday-evening service and organized a prayer meeting outside City Hall, where the crèche would have been.

The performance of the school musical was scheduled for Wednesday, but the producers decided they had enough material with the board meeting, the City Council action and the strife over the manger. Monday morning Phyllis would arrive, and the entire country would get its first glimpse of Hartville, whether it liked it or not.

My column for the Sunday edition did not go over well. I took the last two weeks of programming on the TV talk shows and listed the subject matter for all to see.

Women who fall in love with prisoners.

People who weigh more than four hundred pounds and what they eat.

Elvis sightings. (Betty already had two tapes on order.)

Man who believes his deceased wife came back as a hamster.

Weight loss by alien abduction.

It was a pretty comprehensive list, and not the most flattering. The gist of the article was that we should not necessarily be proud to be in such company. "Town fights over a manger scene" doesn't look as good when it's aired the day before "Children who eat videotape and the parents who love them."

Most people thought I was angry at not being invited to be part of the program. The fact is, I'd gotten the same call as everyone else but decided it simply wasn't my story to tell. Sure, I wrote the column, but as I said, it was only the spark that ignited the powder keg. I was content to sit on the sidelines and observe, which is what a person in my profession is supposed to do anyway.

I could understand the motivation of the atheists. They enjoyed the press. There were so few of them that I figured they needed the publicity. When you're outnumbered and have unpopular views, you jump anytime the light of recognition shines in your corner.

In a way I could understand why the city agreed to be part of the program. In an age when public officials are derided for their lack of activity, they wanted to be seen as on-the-ball leaders, willing to tackle tough issues with a level head. Plus, exposure on national television was something no political figure could refuse.

However, I could not figure out the reaction of the church people. They could only come off looking angry on television and turn off potential converts. They would not mix their manger with Santa and would fight until the plywood Jesus was in his rightful place, alone on the lawn of City Hall. Pluralism was more offensive to them than an outright ban, so the crèche stayed on the sidewalk in front of Wright's Hardware.

From what I knew about religion, church people were supposed to be loving, kind, forgiving folks who reached out to the hurting in the world. In my mind their résumé read something like "Cross-bearing, widow-and-orphan-helping, sin-forgiving, joyful, self-denying, nonjudgmental followers of Jesus."

The Christians of Hartville must not have read the same press release, because they were anything but. I figured if there was a God, and I didn't hold out much hope, he would have to be awfully disappointed in the likes of these people.

But I did know one person who did live up to those ideals: Evelyn, my wife. Though she attended Hartville Community Church, she hadn't said much about the uproar over the column or the protests. She is one of those rare people who have a deep faith and manage not to make you feel like Attila the Hun when you don't share it.

A couple years after Brian was born, she approached me and said she had "accepted Jesus as her personal Savior." I laughed out loud and told her if she wanted to believe in fairy tales it was all right. If it made her feel better to throw her brain out the window she could do it. "Just don't try to make me believe that mush," I said, "and don't give them any of our money." After that she took the girls to church while I watched Brian with one eye and read the Sunday paper with the other.

And she didn't push church on me. I could tell she wanted me to believe, but there were too many unanswered questions for that. I was glad to have a morning of relative peace on Sundays with Brian. When he turned four she started taking him and I stayed by myself.

I'm not saying Evelyn's a saint. She can get beet-red and yell as loud as anybody. But when it came to religion, she was gentle and considerate. She didn't wear Bible-verse T-shirts or play Christian videos with hidden messages. It made me think there was something real about it, at least for her, but I never brought the subject up.

In all those years since her big change, I had never set foot in Hartville Community Church. I felt guilty and a bit awkward when Christmas and Easter rolled around and almost everyone in town slid into a pew somewhere. So it felt strange when I walked in for the first time and saw all the cameras and lights and cables and Phyllis's red hair.

The church held nearly three hundred people on the floor of the sanctuary and another two hundred in the balcony. The room was laid out in a horseshoe configuration, with railings extending from the pulpit to each wall. The pews were wooden and creaked when you sat down, but the place was comfortable. When bathed in the brightness of television, the sign at the front of the platform took on even greater meaning. It said, "You are the light of the world. A city set on a hill cannot be hidden."

Phyllis did not come out until two minutes before airtime. Before that a man named Stan coached us on how to raise our hand if we wanted to say something and how not to talk unless we had a microphone. I guess they had some problems with people not following those rules up in New York, but it seemed pretty logical to me.

The pulpit was removed, and several nice chairs were arranged in a semicircle on the platform. The church was full an hour before the broadcast, and some people scrunched up in the choir loft behind the platform. A few even stood in the empty baptistery to get a glimpse of the audience.

And what an audience it was. Every inch of pew space was filled with an atheist or a Christian or a person who'd seen Jesus in the snowdrift. The mayor was there. The City Council members were there. The school board, all of the teachers, half the parents and even the school choir: it was wall-to-wall Hartvillians.

Pastor Karlsen was enraptured as he gazed at the scene. I could see the wheels of faith spinning in his head, wondering what great things he might be prompted to say in this, the greatest opportunity for evangelism he had ever experienced.

Dierdra Bergman Freep had an equally curious look on her face. It was the first time she had been in a church since her father dragged her there while she was in her teens. She looked like an injured animal caught in a trap, ready to claw someone or chew her own leg off. Or both.

Phyllis pranced out of the pastor's study and waved as the town fawned. You don't think you're actually in awe of someone on television until you see them up close. Makeup powdered her shoulders like fresh snow on a ski slope. I figured the Christians would be the least impressed, since they had boycotted most of the sponsors of Phyllis's programs at one time or another. But when she appeared through the door there was an audible gasp from the room, and several older ladies said, "Aw, there she is," like she was a high-school pal returning for a reunion.

Phyllis now had a production company, had starred in three made-for-television movies and had more money than all of Hartville combined. She had flaming red hair that swished from side to side as she ran back and forth through the audience. She wore several prominent rings and held the microphone just right so they sparkled anytime she held it to her pouting lips.

The theme music blasted through the speakers, and everyone covered their ears except for D. J. Starr. He was smiling and fiddled with his new tie.

The morning sun reflected off the snow and through the stained-glass windows, casting a collage of brilliant colors around the sanctuary. There were poinsettia plants in every corner and huge red bows on the organ and piano at either side of the platform. It was quite homey, I thought, just what Phyllis would want. Like coming home to see relatives, except the relatives were about to kill each other.

I was not allowed to use a transcript of the program for this book. I guess it's one thing to deal with D. J. and Hartville Radio and another to deal with New York. Anyway, as a journalist I do cultivate a rather strong memory, particularly of things like train wrecks, plane crashes and live television programs.

Phyllis welcomed her viewers to beautiful Hartville, looking into the camera one moment and down at her notes the next. She did not use a TelePrompTer but bobbed her head down toward her hand, then up toward the camera as she introduced each guest. She described Hartville as a quaint town with modest vital statistics: a small population, abundant churches and a low crime rate. A videotape inset of the town square rolled on the video monitors, and Phyllis said, "This is the main point of contention in Hartville, because right in the spot you're seeing in the town square, a fifty-year-old tradition has come to an end. And it is mainly because of this woman that you no longer see Mary and Joseph and the baby Jesus lying in the manger."

The monitors quickly cut from the video to a tight shot of the villain. "Her name is Dierdra Bergman Frip," Phyllis said, straining to see her notes. "Is it Frip or Freep?"

"Freep," Dierdra said.

"Freep—I'm sorry," Phyllis said.

There was a tiny ripple of laughter mixed with hisses from the audience, though about a dozen from Atheists Against Mangers began to hoot and clap.

"Why, Dierdra?" Phyllis said, putting her hand behind her head, her neck disappearing. "What's so wrong with a few biblical figurines? Come on, it's Christmas."

Dierdra leaned back like she was about to spit into the wind, then shot forward and released her first volley.

"First of all, I resent having to appear in this place, which is anything but a neutral site," she snarled. Her eyebrows were raised like an angry piano teacher ready to bring the lid down on a student's fingers.

"Secondly, this country has no right to support a religion, be it Christianity or Islam or Buddhism or anything else. The people who began this country came here to get away from state-sponsored religion, and most of the people you see here today want to oppress us with their fundamentalist, Bible-thumping beliefs. They want to shove their morality and their God down our throats, with their plywood Jesus and their small-town Christianity, and we won't stand for it. This country is too great to be taken over by the likes of them."

"Reverend Marty Karlsen is the pastor of Hartville Community Church," Phyllis said quickly. "Reverend, you've been in the middle of things from the start. What's this all about?"

More than anyone on the panel, Karlsen should have felt at home, but a sudden look of fright, almost terror, came over him. His face turned pale and his lower lip quivered slightly as he cleared his throat. I heard someone in the cameraman's headphones say, "Mark an edit." Some areas of the country would see a tighter taped version of our town meeting.

"Phyllis," Karlsen finally said, "what we have here is an age-old battle between good and evil. Between truth and error."

The more he spoke, the more comfortable Karlsen became. An "amen" behind me gave him confidence as he picked up the cadence.

"It's a battle between light and dark. You know, darkness cannot stand the light."

"No," Dierdra interrupted, "we just can't stand your bullying."

"Let him talk," an older voice shouted from the balcony.

"They gave you your turn, now let him have his," another said.

"Go ahead, Reverend," Phyllis said.

"They've actually taken the Bible off the desk of a teacher because they say it endorses religion. I feel sorry for people like Dierdra here who don't have an anchor, who don't have a moral compass for their lives."

"Oh, don't feel sorry for me, Reverend," Dierdra smirked.

"I pray for people like this to . . ."

"Don't waste your prayers on me, Reverend." Each time Dierdra said "Reverend," it sounded like a word used in a shipyard rather than inside a church.

Dierdra and the Reverend were still going at it when the saxophone music swelled and Phyllis put the microphone near her tonsils and said, "And we'll be back."

After the first break Phyllis ran around the church some more and fluffed the back of her hair. When Pastor Karlsen spoke, so did Dierdra. The folks from Atheists Against Mangers hooted, and the rest hissed and booed at them, and I wondered if Phyllis wouldn't cut to the man with the reincarnated hamster before the show was over.

At one point Phyllis, exasperated with the Christians, put one hand on her hip and said, "Reverend, if these people don't want to fa-la-la-la-la with the rest of you, why do you have to force the issue?"

There were some faces on the panel who weren't Hartvillians. I guess the people of Hartville hadn't done well enough on the tests to hold down the show by themselves, so Phyllis and crew brought in some ringers just in case. One was president of the AUSCS, Americans United for the Separation of Crèche and State. Beside her was legal counsel for CCMAD, Concerned Citizens for Manger Displays. Hewitt Lawrence III, impeccably dressed as usual, was on the end, bouncing uncomfortably on his chair. All three looked like the aluminum foil on the top of a hot tin of Jiffy Pop. If they didn't talk soon I thought they would burst and spill out on the poinsettias.

"Here's another perspective to add to the case," Phyllis said, straining to see another tiny note card. "This is Reverend Tal Errant, professor of Bible and psychology at Progressive Theological Seminary located on the West Coast, and author of *Plu-*

ralistic Christianity: Orthodox Hedonism in the Sacred Paradigm. And you say what, sir?"

The professor was the most likable person on the panel, because he seemed to be having the most fun. He smiled and laughed a lot and raised his eyebrows when people hooted and hissed.

He had a thin face, and I could tell his glasses were a great necessity because of their thickness. He looked distinguished but not prudish. Unlike Reverend Karlsen, he wore no tie or any hint of polyester.

"I think this whole discussion is superfluous," Errant said. "We have one side that takes a literal view of the Bible and another side that doesn't want anything to do with religion. The problem is one of inclusion. If Ms. Freep felt heard in her complaints, if her feelings were validated by the other side, she might not be so adamant about her position."

The audience sat slack-jawed, trying to figure out what the professor was saying. Phyllis squeezed her forehead with one hand and shot the microphone to her mouth. "Explain."

"Certainly. The problem with this type of religious expression in the current milieu is its exclusivity. It preaches a stiff, pharisaic gospel that says it alone has the only truth and one must believe the same in order to be in the club.

"We've found it more effective to teach a biblical inclusion for all people. In other words, we boil the Bible down to those things on which everyone agrees, and we emphasize those rather than getting stuck on whether Jesus was born of a virgin or actually raised from the dead.

"For example, we refer to the Being our good Reverend Karlsen would call 'God' as 'Our Eternal Father/Mother' or 'the All Knowing IT.' We emphasize the aspects of the Christmas story that deal with peace, goodwill toward men—excuse me, humans—and we leave out the more offensive aspects for the incarnation-impaired.

"We even have a New Testament for atheists that I'm sure Ms. Freep would benefit from reading. We take out all references to a transcendent deity and replace them with evolutionary terms."

"Could you read a bit of it for us?" Phyllis said.

"Surely. This is the traditional Christmas story from the Gospel of Luke.

The professor poked at his glasses and held the thin book two inches from his face. He read conversationally,

> And there were shepherds, male and female and of all socio-economic strata, nearby, working the third shift with their flocks. And suddenly a shooting star or some other explainable natural phenomenon occurred, and they all had a panic attack. So one of them looked at another and said, "Let's assuage our fears by going down to Bethlehem and finding a baby. Looking at a child renews my faith in humanity."
>
> So they hurried off, praising themselves for such a good idea, and they found Mary and Joseph and the baby, who was lying in the manger, depriving the animals of their rightful place to feed.

"You know, that's what I believe," Phyllis said happily. "I believe God is love and he doesn't care what you call him as long as you're sincere and are a good person and try really hard."

The professor smiled and nodded profusely. Pastor Karlsen tried to say something, but Dierdra interrupted and bedlam ensued. The floor director made a signal, and Phyllis held the microphone close. I strained to hear her as she lowered her voice and punched out over the clamor and music: "Maybe the crux of this town's story is that for too long we've mixed so much religion with Christmas. And we'll be back."

The rest of the program can best be described as controlled mayhem. One guest accused the Christians of being Santa-impaired. Members of the congregation stood to show T-shirts proclaiming "John 3:16," "My Boss Is a Jewish Carpenter" and "Grace Happens" slogans.

One audience member showed her business prowess by publicizing her alternative to "Santa's Workshop." She grabbed the microphone from Phyllis, but Phyllis hung on. It was a furious tug of war, and I thought they were going to get to the top of the microphone, do scissors and throw the thing in the air like a baseball bat, but Phyllis finally regained control and the lady let go.

She was owner of "Yonder Stall Portraits," a manger scene complete with life-size wise men, animals and Jesus' family. For three dollars, children could skip Santa's lap and have their picture taken beside the manger, worshiping the infant King. The audience applauded as she held up an example of her work.

Toward the end of the program the atheists made disparaging remarks about home-schoolers. The Christians brought up the Bible on the desk incident again, and the story of a local boy who was not allowed to pray silently at the lunch table. The parents wanted to sue, and the kid was upset because his pig in a blanket got cold. Another parent complained that high-schoolers were forbidden to kneel in the end zone after a touchdown. From there the credits rolled, and I honestly thought somebody was going to get killed.

When I thought about it later, I remembered that Dierdra's boys were taking in the entire scene—especially the younger one, Rob. He listened to people talk about Christmas and the manger, and for the first time I actually saw him sit still. Of course it's easy to see the beginnings of disaster when you look at it over your shoulder.

6
"WINTER CELEBRATION"

here wasn't much of a "Winter Celebration" at Hartville Elementary School that year. The Christians pulled their kids out of the performance and threatened to never let them come back, vouchers or no vouchers. A couple hundred of them gathered in front of City Hall without the manger. There, led by Deacon Wright, they bellowed out without reserve all the carols that spoke of Jesus, the Lord and the angelic host. There just wasn't anyone there to hear them.

At the school the show went on, but something was missing. A boycott by half the town is tough on third-graders. The teachers were caught in the middle. The administration tsk-tsked and predicted it would all blow over, but it didn't. At least not in time for the performance.

At the concert Frosty had lost most of his "thumpety-thump-thump." Rudolph didn't have his usual zing either. When the kids sang, "Oh you'd better watch out," there was a distinct feeling that we really should. But who should we watch out for, Santa? The church folks? God?

When the program arrived at the humming of "Silent Night," there was an eeriness about the place. You could almost reach out and break the tension like an icicle hanging from the eaves. It seemed to me both groups in Hartville were missing something. Like we'd look back on the end of the year with deep regret.

Until that night the strife in Hartville had not been personal for me. Like any trained professional, I could view the column and resulting recognition it afforded as another person watching from the wings. As I look back, it was like my fathering. I didn't have to participate. I could view it as just another occurrence at my station in life and switch to another channel.

Watching the children on stage, engulfed in the darkness and innocence of childhood, sparked a glimmer of feeling in me. Their faces, so many mouths making such little noise, reached a forgotten part of my soul.

I took a mental journey of Christmas musicals that night. How many times had I sung "Jingle Bells," how many times had parents been encouraged to jangle their keys? No matter how small the part, the fear and anxiety were overwhelming. How I feared making a fool of myself in front of all those kids and all those parents. My parents. I was afraid to sing out in fear I would be off-key, and I was afraid to sing quietly in fear of the director's stern looks. I dreamed I would somehow bring disgrace on our family and forever be listed in the gossip hall of shame in our town. I went over all the possibilities of failure: tripping on the stairs, falling off the risers, forgetting my pants.

Everything came back, including my fervent prayers to a silent

God.

"If only you'll get me through this one night," I pleaded, "if only you'll help me remember these lines. Oh God, please, please help me not to screw this up. Please don't let them laugh at me. I just don't want to be the jerk this year."

And I would bargain with God, things like all my allowance for the next year or a vow to attend church every Sunday and memorize verses and be kind to my siblings and obey everything my mom and dad said. The promises kept mounting with the intensity of the fear.

But no matter how hard I prayed or how much I promised, I couldn't get over the feeling that the Almighty was really ticked off at me. "How many times have you asked this?" I could see him looking over the portals of heaven, like the wizard's face as Dorothy approached. "You sniveling little wretch of a boy, I'll show you!" (Cue thunderbolt.)

Each year something happened. I would forget a word or a phrase or feel I was going to get sick and run off stage or rip my costume or sing through a humiliating quarter rest.

I was a small kid. The few surviving pictures of my youth are scattered images of missing teeth and a broken arm and leg and an occasional gash above an eye. I was clumsy. Awkward. And each year the director strategically placed me on the risers so that my tripping or loss of balance had a cruel domino effect on the rest of the group. And the parents would laugh, and the director would put his hand over his face and shake his head, and the kids would secretly wish me to the art club.

The human derision felt painful, but the crushing blow was the laughter of God. Even as a child I felt his holy "gotcha." Each year I grew further and further from God until I put him away with the rest of Christmas legends, fairy tales and hopes that went unfulfilled. If there was a God, I thought, he was either wholly impotent or massively cruel to the likes of me. This was my conclusion after only a few years of life, and I hadn't even considered global suffering.

A thousand pictures flashed through my mind as I watched those kids sing. I remembered my anticipation of the Rudolph special on television. The first year it came on there was unbridled fascination with Clarice and Yukon Cornelius and Hermy who wanted to be a dentist. I was thrilled with the Abominable Snowman and a bit puzzled by the dysfunctional Santa whose wife constantly stuffed him and criticized his lack of weight gain.

Television bound our family together at Christmas. A ball of light glowed in every Hartvillian window as the Grinch made his way down to Whoville with his dog Max. Down to the houses where all the men looked like C. Everett Koop.

I thought about Charlie Brown's Christmas tree. The voices of those kids in that first Christmas special were perfect, could never be matched again. Little Linus with his nasal voice, wrapped in a blanket as a shepherd, told Charlie Brown he wasn't a blockhead for choosing the ugliest tree. I suppose the feeling I got from that cartoon has stuck with me my entire life.

The images of childhood sometimes yield tradition, so on Christmas Eve I gather the kids and we sit in front of the television with a fresh tub of popcorn. The kids are dressed in pajamas, their hair still wet from the bath. The scent of unrinsed baby shampoo fills the air. We sit together as a family and watch one of these old programs. One year it's the Grinch. The next we pull out Alistair Sim's portrayal of Ebenezer Scrooge. We share the transformation each story brings, whether it's the voice of Boris Karloff or Jimmy Stewart playing George Bailey or old

Ebenezer. We share the warmth and love of Bob Cratchit for Tiny Tim.

And then the year came back, locked away in a forgotten part of my soul. The year I wept. As the Ghost of Christmas Future showed Scrooge the shadows of things that were to come, I wept. These were shadows that had already materialized in our own lives.

I watched my two daughters in the gymnasium of Hartville Elementary performing safe songs in a politically correct culture, and I felt the shoe of my son Brian slapping against my leg, then banging on the folding chair. Back and forth, back and forth, thud, bang, thud, bang. My Brian, such a wounded little Tim.

Seven years earlier we had rejoiced over the news of twins soon to be born. Lily and Kelly bubbled with excitement, and Evelyn was nesting for two, cleaning and rinsing everything she could find. I think she even washed the dirt in the back yard. The preparations were like Christmas. We cleared the spare room and bought two cribs. I splattered the walls with sky-blue Dutch Boy and allowed Evelyn to stencil a border of pink bears on parade. We would be a large family, something Evelyn had dreamed about, and I would have a son. At least I thought the odds were pretty good.

During the early stages of labor, something went wrong. I was ushered out of the delivery room, and Brian was taken quickly to surgery. Brian's tiny sister—I could have held her in the palm of one hand—never took a breath of air. We named her Rachel, a little lamb never warmed by her mother's love.

Brian was stronger and struggled from his mother's womb. But when the doctor came to me, his mask pulled from his face like a dirty napkin, I could tell my little boy would need more than a crutch and a rich benefactor whose priorities had changed.

Perhaps Brian's brain damage was more difficult for me to face than his physical problems. I wanted to teach my son baseball and football. I wanted to share stories and pocketknives and his first glove. But that day I held a broken son, a damaged life. It was terrible thinking I would never coach his Little League team, but it was the thought that I would never be able to break through into Brian's world that crushed me. Words were my life. I put them on paper and sent them into the world. I scattered words the way a farmer scatters seeds in a field. But I would not share many words with Brian, and I could not enter his dull world of sight and sound.

There were numerous surgeries. Evelyn worked with him each day, and eventually he learned to walk and could actually run with a shuffling motion. We found ways to communicate. We understood thirst. We knew his sign of hunger and fatigue. But there was no communication on any deeper level, nothing more than a word or two, and I knew the same "gotcha" had struck again in my life. The domino had tumbled onto our family, this time with lasting effects. I would not look at my son for seven years without thinking of the cruelty of God. In those years, I never saw Brian without thinking of God's anger toward me and the human race.

I tasted Christmas that night at the Winter Celebration. I tasted all my Christmases as if they were rolled into a huge ball of snow and thrown at me by a mean-spirited deity. I turned in time to get hit full in the face. I tasted Christmas through my children again, watching them sing and dance pathetically, seeing myself again and not able to turn away. I saw each of us as a Cratchit or a Tim or an empty chair, only this was not a story from long ago. It was life. It was now.

My breath floated before me in the cold like Christmas memories, and we drove home silently with our children. Outside, houses brightly dotted the landscape with their decorations. The smell of little chocolates, mints and striped candy canes rose from the back seat.

"You guys were good tonight," I said.

Nothing came but the sound of little mouths busy with candy.

"You sure were," Evelyn said. "We were both real proud of you."

Chew, chew, suck, crackle . . . crunch.

"Brian, don't bite the candy cane, bud," I said. "You're supposed to just hold it in your mouth."

Crunch, crunch, crunch, crunch.

7

THE CHRISTMAS EVE CRISIS

orld War I came to a halt one Christmas. The story says soldiers in the midst of furious battles laid down their arms for a day of peace. They ate their meager rations together and exchanged small gifts.

It was not so in Hartville. The verbal Scud missiles continued. Someone hung two angels from the cedars at City Hall. They were taken down the next day and in their place was a note that said, "Unapproved expression of sentiment toward religious holidays is strictly forbidden."

People settled into the Yuletide routine, but the animosity was thick. You could have measured it by the pound as Christians passed the town square. By Christmas weekend it was clear that Hewitt Lawrence III had failed the faithful. In a conversation with Pastor Karlsen, the lawyer expressed deep regret that there were other cases that would take him to the Supreme Court faster and he was going to concentrate on them. Perhaps that was when the change in Karlsen began.

The weather turned colder, and grown children came to town to spend the holidays with their families. The people of Hartville enjoyed food and friends and did their best to put the conflict behind them.

On the Friday before Christmas a group from the Community Church moved the crèche from the front of Wright's Hardware to Hartville Park on Grace Avenue. They were having trouble getting the wise men to stay in a standing position and were forced to lean them against parking meters, which was a violation of a city ordinance against foot traffic impedance. The whole scene was soon loaded onto the back of a pickup and given a police escort to the second-base area of the softball field in the little park. It was not a happy day for the Christians, but they conceded that the crèche was becoming a hazard on Main Street, what with all the honking and people stepping over the fallen wise men.

Christmas Eve fell on a Sunday that year, and Evelyn took the girls to the church's candlelight service. I stayed with Brian and watched *It's a Wonderful Life*. We planned to play a shorter video when the girls returned, but as it turned out, we didn't watch anything together that year.

Evelyn turned as they were leaving. "You know you're welcome to come with. You're always welcome."

I nodded and folded my arms, my navy-blue sweater bunching underneath. "I'll stay with him," I said. "It's safer here tonight, I think."

Evelyn liked taking Brian with her. The girls loved to see him dressed up, and families at the church made a general fuss over his presence. But I was using Brian that year, as I had done when he was younger, to escape even the possibility of attending a service.

I *was* curious about the pastor's message. He had come by the office early Saturday while I finished a column and tidied my desk. He looked subdued, almost contrite, as he shuffled across the Elvis throw rug in Betty's office and came to my door to shake my hand.

"We'd love to see you at the service tomorrow night, Jack. I think you'd find it quite interesting. Maybe even get another column out of it."

"I appreciate that, Pastor, but the last time I came, I didn't know if I'd make it out in one piece. Is there a wrestling match this year, or the same old hymns and a sermon?"

"No." Karlsen smiled. "It's an intriguing idea though. I'll have to give the wrestling match some thought."

Karlsen turned serious, his brow inching closer to his eyes.

"Evelyn will be there with the girls, I suppose."

"I suppose."

"I hope you never take her for granted, Jack."

He said it in such a preachy tone, like I had never considered what a wife I had. But he *was* a preacher, so I bit my lip and tried to smile.

"Well," Karlsen said, "we would love to have you. It's going to be a service the whole town won't forget."

I couldn't stand one more thing I couldn't forget, so I opted for Jimmy Stewart and Donna Reed, a pleasant memory. I actually had never seen *It's a Wonderful Life* until the weekend after our wedding. Evelyn had insisted we watch it together by candlelight. I can still remember that little black-and-white television with the rabbit ears. In those days the movie was on every station in half-hour increments, so we picked the one with the clearest reception and settled under the covers, a candle flickering on top of the television. For this reason that film has taken on special meaning through the years.

I sat Brian in his chair by the hearth. A fire was crackling, and the wood smoke smelled heavenly. Like a scratch-and-sniff Norman Rockwell. Brian liked to sit and watch the embers glow. Every now and then he put his hand out to feel the heat and then smiled.

I turned on the VCR and he watched, his head swaying back and forth like a doll's. I wondered what was going on in his mind. Did he know anything about me other than the word *Dada*? Could he comprehend the change of seasons and the reason there was a tree in our living room with brightly wrapped presents underneath? He could say individual words and even associate them correctly. *TV* was a favorite—upon hearing it he generally rushed down the stairs to the family room. He knew *dinner* and *lunch* and *Jesus*, which came out "deenuw" and "lutch" and "Deesus."

"This is one of my favorite movies of all time," I said to him gently. I talked this way often when we were alone, his head swaying to my voice. "It's the story of George Bailey and all the people who were changed by his life. He didn't understand what a difference he had made."

Brian seemed to perk up at different points in the film. When the children went shovel sledding, he cooed and put a hand to his mouth. When the high-school dance led to the swimming-pool scene, he seemed to laugh, his mouth open wide and an "ahhhhh" sound coming forth.

I saw a look of connection in his face—then, realizing he needed a change of diaper, I felt foolish. Every parent of a disabled child has the same hope. You dream of a breakthrough experience like Helen Keller's with the water. I held hope that Brian would suddenly scratch a word in the sandbox and let us know he understood everything we said and did for him. But that day hadn't come and never would, I thought.

I changed him and sat down with a cup of coffee. George was at the prayer scene, pleading with God to show him the way. Clarence would be along soon as an answer to that prayer, and I thought about all the times my feeble petitions had fallen on deaf ears.

Voices outside stirred me from my chair, and I went to the front window. Our home is not far from Main Street and only a couple of blocks from the church. Evelyn and the girls had walked there, but it was much too early for them to be back.

I opened the drapes and beheld an amazing sight. A stream of candles poured down the church steps onto the sidewalk—all the little yellow lights running to and fro, then extinguished by the biting wind. There was a knock at the door, and I glanced at Brian before answering it. He was looking at the fireplace again, his hand stretched toward the warmth.

"Jack, you're not going to believe it," Betty Stanton said as I opened the door. A cold blast shot through the entry and my sweater too. "You're just not going to believe it."

"Come on inside, Betty."

"There's no time. I've got to get back right away and help."

"Help who? What's going on?"

"It happened at the church."

"*You* went to church?" I said in disbelief.

"I went because of the pastor," she frowned. "He came to the office yesterday and said he was going to make an announcement tonight about the manger wars."

"So it was a working religious experience." I laughed.

"This is serious, Jack. Dierdra Freep's kid is missing."

My mouth dropped. "Which one?"

"The little one that bounces off everything. Rob, I think."

"Yeah, Rob's the younger one."

"The pastor had just started his speech or sermon or—oh, whatever you call it—and Dierdra came running inside. Everything stopped, I mean everything. You could have heard a Communion wafer drop. She was sobbing and said the little fellow had disappeared twenty minutes earlier. The front door was open and his coat was gone."

"And that's where everyone's going, to look for him?"

"Except your wife. She sat Dierdra down to warm her up with some coffee. The poor thing was out in the weather with only a sweater. Didn't even take time to get her own coat."

I looked back at Brian, who was still by the fire, swaying aimlessly like a toy horse.

"I'm headed out with the rest to look," Betty said. "We could sure use your help."

"I'd like to, but I have Brian with me," I said, but Betty was already chugging down the steps toward Main Street. I could see her breath puffing like smoke from a steam locomotive. It would mean serious work on the sidewalk if she fell.

I ran my fingers through my hair and cursed. Something in me wanted to be the hero and find the boy, but with Brian it seemed impossible. I went downstairs and turned off the television.

"Hey buddy, you want to go for a walk with me?"

Brian stared at the fire.

"Outside?" I said.

He turned, and the look on his face showed he understood. Brian loved anything outside. "Outside" meant playing in dirt and eating it and sitting in sand. He shot past me in a shuffle, heading toward the closet. Dressing Brian for winter weather is as easy as putting socks on a walrus. But this night he watched quietly as I zipped his snowsuit and pulled his hat over his ears. I stood him up, and his arms stuck out from his body. He looked just like any other kid going out to play.

Unfortunately, I couldn't find Brian's shoes; this dilemma was not uncommon, but presented a great problem in this particular situation. I looked by the fireplace, then flew into the closet in a frenzy, but came up empty. Then I remembered seeing house shoes for Brian and the girls in Evelyn's closet. They were wrapped and under the tree, and I opened two packages before I found his. They were fluffy, foamy shoes called Snugglers, made by the Snuggle Slipper Factory.

"New shoes," I said, jamming them on his feet, the wrapping paper all around us. They looked comfortable but wouldn't last a minute in the snow. I threw on my coat and put Brian on my shoulder.

The night was blue. Stars sprinkled the sky, and the moon was already high above us. It made stick shadows of the trees against the snow. I could hear voices yelling as I turned toward the church. Others were moving down Main Street, so I headed west along Grace.

Brian put his face next to mine. I could feel his breath against my neck, warm and soft. Every few steps he sniffed, and the sniffing was getting wetter and wetter. I pulled a handkerchief from my pocket and wiped his nose. I told him to blow, but he did not understand.

We turned down Grace and came near the manger scene, now deserted. Gaudy Christmas lights, blue, red and white, surrounded the lean-to and cast a department-store shine on the scene. If you looked at the crèche from just the right angle and from enough distance, you might have thought the construction quaint and sturdy. But from the side you could see that Mary, Joseph and the three wise men were simply plywood cutouts. Whoever had painted them did not grasp the form of the human face. The eyes were too close on Joseph, too far apart on Mary. The gift of gold came in bars like you would see in Fort Knox. The other two wise men held weird-looking boxes. I thought it a gift the artist had not attempted to render frankincense and myrrh.

The manger was crudely built, which actually was refreshingly realistic. It was simply an animal trough with hay brimming over the sides. The animals had been donated by Henderson's World of Ceramics on the edge of town, so there was an abundance of geese, deer and even a flamingo, but only one tired-looking sheep and a pig with a rather smarmy look on his face. This was a Hartville manger. This was what all the fuss was about.

We were half a block away and heading toward Maple when Brian spied the sight and grabbed my neck. "Main-nuw," he said, trying to say *manger*. "Main-nuw."

If Brian had been walking, I would have been able to give a few sharp tugs on his hand to bring him along. I probably would have put myself between him and the lighted scene to our left and shielded him, but because he was wearing his Snugglers and in my arms, he came, he saw, he wiggled. Veni, vidi, viggli.

"We can't see the manger right now, bud. There's a little boy out in the cold, and we need to find him."

"Main-nuw," he said, a little louder.

I wiped his nose again and continued toward Maple. If little Rob was hiding in his mother's basement, I would kill him, I thought.

"Main-nuw!" Brian screamed. My son is not a vocal child, but when he wants something there is very little that will stop him.

"We *can't* go to the manger, Brian. *We can't*. DO YOU UNDERSTAND? *NO*. I SAID NO!"

His nose was dripping again, and I wiped it dry. I couldn't remember yelling at him that way, and something inside felt crushed that I had.

"Main-nuw," he said softly.

I knelt down and held him on my knee. He was smaller than most seven-year-olds, but still a bundle to carry. I pushed a tear across his red cheek. We had been outside only a few minutes, but already the cold was taking its toll. I had no gloves, and my hands stung as if pine needles were being pushed into them. I wondered what kind of condition Rob Freep would be in if he truly was out in the weather.

"Buddy, I can't make you understand this, but Daddy has something really important to do. We can't go to the manger."

For the longest time he looked back at me, straight in the eye, no swaying. Then he said again softly, "Main-nuw."

I picked him up and moved past a huge oak tree, toward the first house that would block the manger from our view.

"When we get back home we'll make some hot chocolate and have a snack," I said. Then I said the word *snack* again a little louder, as a mantra of good behavior. "Snack. Snack. *Snack*."

"Main-nuw."

I did not want Brian to win this battle, for I knew the war was fought on beachheads like this one. If I stood firm during these small skirmishes, I would eventually win the war. But I felt so bad about yelling at him that I finally turned around and hurried toward the crèche.

"We're going to freeze to death anyway," I said. "Might as well enjoy the view.

"Look, buddy," I continued, "we can't stay at the manger." I knew he would cry harder when we had to leave. That's the thing about giving in: you retreat one step and the enemy grabs another hill. "We'll look at it for a minute and then we have to go, okay? Understand, bud?"

"Main-nuw," he said.

Clumps of snow fell from the trees as we walked into the open field where the blinking manger lay. The cold stung my eyes until they watered, and the scene blurred. I chuckled to myself as I thought this would be the closest I would come to a church on Christmas Eve. I would worship at a plywood Jesus with a broken little boy who had no idea what he was seeing.

We were a few yards away when I saw something in the manger. I shook my head and squinted. Was it an animal in there? No, it looked like clothing of some sort. A body.

"Main-nuw," Brian said.

"What in the world?" I said.

I heard my feet crunch through the snow. Second base was lower than the rest of the field, and the snow had blown deep. I felt it go over the tops of my shoes and sting my legs above the sock line.

The manger was a long, deep trough, and you could not see fully inside until you came close to the edge. There was Mary, looking in two directions at the same time. Joseph stood beside her with a bewildered visage. One wise man held a gold brick.

A mist rose from my mouth as I panted, the extra weight of Brian taking my breath. Together we peered over the edge of the manger, and I saw shoes and jeans and a coat and the frosted face of Rob Freep. His eyes were closed tight, and his hands looked blue in the moonlight.

I did not want Brian to see him. The sight of death might disease his already damaged mind. But before I could turn away, Brian spoke.

"Deesus," he said excitedly. "Deesus!"

I can't explain the feeling at that moment of seeing the body of that little child so still and lifeless. If he had been sacrificed in some pagan ritual it would not have been more terrifying.

But when Brian spoke, the frozen child blinked. Then Rob miraculously opened his eyes and sat up amidst the straw. He put both hands on the manger's edge and looked curiously at us.

"Are you okay?" I said, shivering.

"Who are you?" Rob said.

"We heard you were lost and came to look for you. Everybody's looking for you."

His eyes darted from one face to the other, then around the manger scene. It was as if he had fallen asleep and we were trespassers in his bedroom, though someone had definitely turned down the heat.

"Why are you out here?" I said.

Rob thrust out his chin and looked up at me. He still had both hands on the manger. Straw hung from the arms of his coat.

"I wanted to see."

"See what?"

"See what it's like to be Jesus," he said.

There was an uncomfortable pause as I processed his words. Did he mean he wanted more information about the real Jesus, the one his mother was so adamantly against? Or did he just want to see what lying in a cow stall was like in the middle of winter?

"Well," I said after a few moments, "how does it feel?"

Rob blew into his little cupped hands and rubbed them together. "It feels pretty cold," he said.

"Do you want to go home?"

"Yes sir."

I helped him up out of the manger and saw the plywood Jesus underneath. Rob brushed the hay from the wooden baby's face.

"Do you think you can walk?" I said.

"Yeah, I got here okay, I can walk back."

"How long have you been out here?"

"I don't know."

We struggled back through the deep snow, the wind beating our faces, taking our breath away. It had been there throughout our walk, but I had not realized it until I turned toward home. Brian hadn't said anything since he had seen the live boy step out of the manger. He looked over my shoulder at the bright scene receding. "Main-nuw," he said softly. "Main-nuw."

This was not a plea but recognition, I thought. There was something important my son had seen that everyone else had missed. Someone once said that if I knew everything going on in the mind of my child I might be astounded, but no one had ever mentioned the things going on in his heart.

Compared to Brian physically, I am an Olympic athlete. But deep under all my layers of opinion and sarcasm, underneath all the years of trying not to feel, there is a cold heart. A dead heart. Compared with my child, my low-quality-of-life son who looks at a manger with wonder, I am among the walking dead, and I realized it that Christmas Eve. I saw a dilapidated display fashioned from cheap wood and covered with snow. He saw beyond them to God made flesh, the infant King.

I held Rob's hand and squeezed Brian tightly to my shoulder until we came to my house. I had forgotten to lock the front door, and it stood open, the light from inside spilling out on the porch. The motion-sensor light above the garage clicked on as we started up the steps, and someone rushed through the living room. Evelyn opened the storm door anxiously.

"Jack, Dierdra's son is missing and everyone's out looking . . ."

Her voice trailed off as I glanced down at him, his hand high in the air clutching mine. "Oh dear God," she said and grabbed him in her arms. "Thank you, Jesus."

"Dierdra!" she yelled as she ran to the kitchen.

I saw Dierdra Bergman Freep round the corner, a paper towel twisted in a knot around her hand. In a crisis people will use the strangest things for comfort. Dierdra looked as if someone had kicked her in the stomach, but when she saw Rob, her mouth dropped open, and for the first time I saw her break into a regular, human smile. She grabbed the kid and held him so tight I thought his head would pop off.

Evelyn cried, and Lily and Kelly jumped around the room. Brian even picked up on the feeling and started to "ahhhhhhh."

I felt something on my cheek and reached to wipe it away. I caught myself before I touched it and consciously let it slide down the length of my face. It left a streak of water that came close to the corner of my mouth but then turned slightly and hung on the edge of my chin. I felt it drop and heard the slight tick as it hit and skidded down the polyester surface of my coat. It was my first act of defiance of my former life. The first moment of conscious feeling—not the crying, but letting that tear descend and fall wherever it pleased.

The women took Rob and Brian to the fireplace and wrapped them with blankets and hot-water bottles. I stood in the entry of our home, feeling for the first time. Sensing things I had long believed were impossible.

Betty ran up the stairs behind me and nearly knocked me over. "Is he here?" she panted.

"He's here, Betty."

I told her where we had found him, and she talked with Dierdra a few moments. Then she called the police and the church—something I had forgotten to do. She trudged back to the front door then, as if her mission were not yet complete.

"You did real good tonight, Jack," she said.

"Real well," I corrected, smiling.

"Funny," she snapped, and then with a sigh said, "I'm headed back to the office. Everybody's going to want to read about this tomorrow."

"Betty, it's Christmas Eve. Those papers were printed an hour ago."

"I know. Maybe I'll have them run it again. Or maybe we can put out an extra cover page or print up a single sheet and stuff it in. I don't know, we just need to tell them about tonight."

"Can't it wait until Tuesday?" I said. "It'll still be news Tuesday, won't it?"

"No, everybody will want to know what happened. And besides, the pastor says he's holding a special Christmas service for the whole town. Jack, what he started to say before Dierdra came in . . ."

Betty had a strange look on her face. There was something stirring in her as well.

"What? What did he say?"

"I suggest you show up tomorrow and find out for yourself. I've got work to do. Good night."

8
THE MESSAGE

o sugarplums danced in the heads of my children that Christmas Eve. All three slept like rocks until Christmas morning. We skipped the movie because of all the excitement, but continued the tradition of Dad making pancakes for everyone as they opened their stockings at the breakfast table. As usual, I was as surprised as the kids at most of their presents, and I felt bad that Evelyn had done all the shopping. I vowed that would change in years to come.

I put a recording of Evelyn's favorite Christmas songs in the cassette player and turned it low. I protest hymns or Christian music any other day of the year but allow my family this simple pleasure on Christmas morning.

There's something about a Christmas Day that doesn't like the out of doors. Christmas Day was meant for inside, the warmth of the kitchen, the smell of the fireplace mixed with the turkey or ham, spilled pancake mix getting hard on the kitchen counter, the excitement of unwrapped packages, a mountain of wrapping paper and boxes and the squeals of happy children.

I remember my father sitting cross-legged on the couch at Christmas, my grandfather next to him, his face rough with a two-day-old beard. They stood to light their pipes and looked out the window. They talked of the weather or something going on in government, and the tobacco smoke swirled around them like memories that float in the mind and saturate every part of you. That was the last Christmas we would have with my grandfather. I've carried that picture in my head each Christmas since, and I swear I can still smell the Sir Walter Raleigh.

I stood at our window holding a huge piece of fudge, much too health-conscious for a pipe. The day was white, and every now and then a car passed filled with children and presents and parents fighting in the front seat. They were obviously arguing because one of them believed there was something about Christmas that didn't like to be in a car driving to a relative's house.

I looked out at the lawn through the icicles that hung from the eaves and felt an overwhelming sense of loss, as if I had wasted so many years with anger at God and complacency toward my family. I had tried hard to become a professional and set goals and reach for stars, but when I made it to my stars they were pale in comparison with what I now felt was important.

I counted thirty-nine icicles hanging from the eaves, the same number as my own age. Thirty-nine long, impressive cylinders of nothing but water. Drips from a dirty trough. If I had taken my hand and run it across them, breaking them off at the base, I would have no more wasted them than I had my own life.

It is a very sad thing when a man finds, in the middle of his existence, that he has no real life at all. But sadder still is the one who discovers it and does not change.

The service was scheduled for 11:00 that morning. It was a strategic move on Pastor Karlsen's part, allowing enough time for the kids to open presents and get sufficiently bored with the loot. He knew all the cooks in the congregation had their roasts in by 10:00 a.m. and wouldn't be taking them out until 1:00, just before the football game. The rolls were buttered and covered with foil, and the potatoes only had to be heated and whipped. With the excitement of the evening before, Karlsen knew that many would show up who hadn't darkened the church's door since the previous year.

Most of Hartville had read the story inserted hastily by Betty. I counted three spelling errors and a couple of run-on sentences, but otherwise she had done a good job of conveying the urgency of the story. I came out looking a little less than a knight in shining armor and could only imagine what Phyllis would have done with the unfolding drama. What the town didn't know was the identity of the real hero: my son, Brian. It felt good to turn those words over in my mind. *My son.*

The church was absolutely packed. Betty Stanton would have had to lose fifty pounds to wedge one other Hartvillian into the Community Church. And it wasn't just church attenders who were there. It was people from the town who had been on the sidelines of the debate, unwilling to take sides. It was people who wore Christian T-shirts sitting next to atheists who couldn't stand the thought of the crèche on public ground. They were all people who had worked together the night before to find a little boy lost in the cold, and what they believed about mangers and words in songs took a back seat when a life was at stake.

The only one I didn't see was Dierdra, and, well, you couldn't half blame her for not showing up, given all that had happened.

I sat with one hand in Evelyn's, an arm around Brian and both eyes on Lily and Kelly, who suddenly looked very grown-up. There were young, hormonally challenged boys all around us, and it was all I could do to not slap each one and tell them my girls weren't getting married till they were in their forties.

The cynic in me said Pastor Karlsen was going to use the opportunity to preach hellfire and brimstone. At last, with no advertising blitz, Sunday-school competition or New York talk show to shape the sermon, he had a huge crowd in his church. It was a crowd that needed salvation, as far as I could tell. And as in the days of my youth, I figured there would be a couple of songs, a sermon on John 3:16 and an altar call, complete with "Just As I Am" being sung fifty times and Pastor Karlsen saying, "We're going to sing it just one more time to give you a chance to come down to the front of the church. Don't put it off." Something like that.

To my surprise, he didn't do anything like that. The organist was playing a somber version of what I later found out was called "Let the Walls Fall Down." When it was over, a nicely dressed Deacon Wright came to the pulpit and held onto it like it was the last life raft on the *Titanic*. He looked confused, and I couldn't help thinking there was some sort of disagreement between him and the pastor over what was about to happen.

"This is a special day in Hartville," the deacon said. The sound system emitted a high-pitched squeal, and Deacon Wright cupped his hand over the microphone, which only made it worse. I looked to the back of the auditorium at a teenager who was fiddling with knobs and buttons on the sound board.

"Tommy, just set it and leave it alone," Deacon Wright bellowed. The squeal went away, and Tommy's face looked like a chili pepper with rouge.

"This is a special day," Wright continued, "because a little boy that was lost has been found."

"Amen," a man said in front.

"It's special because we celebrate the birth of another little boy in Bethlehem nearly two thousand years ago.

"Pastor Karlsen and I talked about this service, which was supposed to be last night, and you all know what happened last night. We talked about it Friday after our radio broadcast. And I'll admit, we've had our problems over it. But for some reason the Lord has allowed all this to happen, and I think we ought to hear our pastor out. So for those who haven't been here in a while and are nervous, we aren't going to make you sing a solo or anything. We're not passing the plate for an offering, though it pains me a bit with everybody here."

A ripple of relief disguised as laughter spread through the auditorium, and Deacon Wright smiled. I could sense people leaning forward, as if in great anticipation for what lay ahead.

There is a feeling you get in a church, one that I had not experienced since I was a kid. It's a feeling that everything is right with the world. A feeling that you can relax. I settled into the hard pew, and some part of me felt good for being there. Like I was doing my duty. I was sitting through a sermon again and could afford an extra slice of pie or stretching out before the television with no guilt. I was paying my penance by just being there, and it felt good.

Wright stepped back. The crowd hushed as Pastor Karlsen came to the pulpit.

"Thank you, Deacon Wright," Karlsen said. "We *have* had our differences over the past couple of days, because I want to begin by saying we're sorry. To every one of you that we've called names or spoken harshly against in this community, I say we're sorry. To everyone, especially the fellow who was playing Santa Claus and his elves who got banged up, we want to say we're sorry. To the teachers and the administrators and the school board and the workers at City Hall and the mayor, we want to say we're sorry."

I glanced around the platform through the stillness. An American flag stood proudly to the pastor's left, the Christian flag to his right. Every star and stripe seemed to listen.

"Sorry for what?" Karlsen continued. "I think that's what every member of this congregation is asking right now. We put our hearts and souls into getting that manger back in the public square, and we fought till the very end. So what are we sorry for? Sorry for standing up for what's right? Sorry for trying to get God back in the schools where he belongs? No. There's a time to take a stand and a way to take a stand, and I'm telling you here today, on this Christmas morning, that our cause was right.

"But Jesus said, 'Love your enemies and pray for those who persecute you,' and that's where we were wrong. We did it wrong and we're sorry.

"I wish those cameras were back here from New York. I'd look right into their little red lights and I'd tell Phyllis and the panel and the whole country that we were wrong. We're sorry."

I sat with my mouth open, unable to breathe or move. Brian swayed at my side, taking my arm with him.

"We wanted to be salt and light, my friends, but we poured our salt into an open wound, and we took a blowtorch to this town. We are told to love others because he first loved us. If we say we love God but hate others, we're fooling ourselves."

Deathly silence was interrupted by rustling and a few whispers. I turned to see the door to the narthex close and someone slip into the very last row. Pastor Karlsen looked up, then stepped back from the pulpit.

"And I want to say right now," he continued, moving down past the altar and to the first pew, speaking without the aid of a microphone, "that there's one person I am particularly glad to see here today."

Tommy was frantic in the back, but Karlsen waved him off and kept walking. Though his normal voice reminded me of Mr. Haney, his preaching voice carried to the back of the room. Every head followed him as if it was the final tie-breaking point at Wimbledon.

"I don't mean to make a spectacle here, and it's probably the last thing she would want me to do, but when I saw her come in I knew I had to make one special apology, and that is to you, Dierdra. We have talked about you at our dinner tables. We have poisoned our children by calling you names, and we've turned them against your wonderful little boys. I don't care how wrong we think you may be about the manger, or how wrong we think you are about the public schools: what we have done is not right. It is not!"

"Amen," said a hundred voices in the congregation, staggered just enough to make it sound like a thousand.

"When your little boy turned up missing last night, Dierdra, it was clear as day to me that we had missed the boat. And thank God we put aside our differences for his sake."

Karlsen shook his head and put his hand over his mouth. His back was turned to me, but I could tell a wellspring of emotion was breaking forth. He moved back toward the front of the church, his lips pinched firmly shut as if he were holding a finger in a dike.

"Preacher," a voice called from behind him. "I accept your apology. For my son, and my whole family, I accept it. And I want to thank you and everybody who helped me find him. You didn't have to, but you did."

Karlsen turned, raced back to Dierdra Bergman Freep, who was now standing, and gave her the biggest hug I have ever seen a man of the cloth give to an atheist. There were many "amens" now and a lot of sniffling and wiping of eyes.

Finally Karlsen moved back to the pulpit. He wiped his eyes and forehead, then replaced the handkerchief in his breast pocket.

"I don't have any of this written down," he said. "But I want to tell you all something. You can have the best intentions, you can have truth and God on your side, and still be wrong.

"Listen to me. We were so caught up with our constitutional rights and our legal protections under the law and our convictions about freedom of religion that we forgot about the most important thing Christmas came to bring. A relationship.

"We were so high and mighty about the manger. We fought a culture war to keep God in the center of Christmas, and we let him get out of the center of our own lives.

"Let me say this to you. We can win legal battles all the way to the Supreme Court, but if we lose a soul, everything we've done will have been in vain."

I had never seen Pastor Karlsen preach, but judging from the congregation, they hadn't seen him this exercised in a while. Deacon Wright sat with his arms folded and a slight scowl on his face. There were several black members who were now rocking back and forth harder than Brian, ready to swing a handkerchief or two. "That's right," one of them said. "You know it."

"Friends," Karlsen said, "and I'm talking to members of this congregation and others who call themselves Christians, how many of us in here are for prayer in the schools? How many of you want the Ten Commandments back on the walls of our class-rooms? Go ahead, raise your hands. Put them up there high so everybody can see them."

About 95 percent of the crowd raised a hand.

"That's good. That's wonderful. Now put your hands down. We've really got a consensus here, haven't we?"

"Amen!"

"That's right."

"You know it."

"Now let me ask you another question. How many of those who just said they were for prayer in the school—how many of you prayed with your children last night before they went to bed? How many of you prayed with them at the breakfast table before they went off to school last week, or prayed with them at the dinner table, more than to thank the Almighty for the food and bless it to the nourishment of our bodies?"

Apparently either everyone thought it a rhetorical question or they had just been nailed by the pastor, because no one raised a finger.

"How many of you right now can give me more than five of the Ten Commandments? Go on, think about it. Can you name them right now?

"It's easy to hold a poster or wear a T-shirt, but it's harder to really live what you believe.

"Now I've been talking to myself here the last few minutes as much as anybody. I got caught up in the fight and got swept along like a lot of you on both sides. But the whole thing comes down to this: if we believe that the God of the universe invaded time and space for us, how far will we go to communicate his message to others? How much love will we show to people who are against us?

"The message of Christmas is this, friends. The same little baby who felt the straw in the manger felt the nails on the cross. The same baby those smelly old shepherds came to see was the very Lamb of God who came to take away our sins. And if we can sit here being forgiven by the holy God of the universe, and turn around and spit venom at the people who don't know him, then God help us. We've missed it, friends. We've missed the whole reason for Christmas."

Pastor Karlsen was sweating profusely. He loosened his tie for more air. The congregation was still now. What Karlsen said next was to me. I was convinced at the time that he had read my diary, though I've never kept one.

"I've been talking about those in the church who call themselves Christians, and I know there are some of you who don't call yourselves that. I say this a lot and I mean it: I am the biggest sinner in this room. I know more about the Bible than most here, and I get paid to study and expound the Word, and the more I read, the more I see how holy God is and how sinful I am.

"The truth is, we're all in the same boat. We are all sinful, and I know that's not a politically correct term, but it's true. He has every right to cast us away and every right to drop-kick us through the goalposts of eternal punishment. Just one sin could do that, let alone the hundred I commit every day."

"Preach it."

"You know it."

"Amen."

"But you know what? Here's the good news about Christmas. Are you listening?"

"We're listening, Lord," a voice behind me said.

"God isn't mad at you anymore," Pastor Karlsen said. "*God isn't mad at you anymore!* Do you know that? Do you believe that?"

A smile came across Karlsen's face like a golden sunrise on a spring morning. "The Father who has every right to punish you sent his Son to die for you. And that's how I know he's not mad at you, my friend."

I bent my head and thought of all the ways God had been mad at me. All the unanswered prayers, all the holy "gotchas" of my life, rolled together into a huge knot inside my heart. Could there be a chance that God was real? Did such a being care for me?

I had pictured God with folded arms, tapping foot and a look of disdain, but this man said the Father was holding out his hands ready to embrace me.

Evelyn put her hand on my shoulder.

"I wish we could have put that manger up in front of City Hall where it had been for fifty years," Karlsen said. "But more than that, I wish I would have honored Christmas in my heart. I wish I would have shown a little bit of the love and understanding God showed me when he forgave me. I wish I would have done less talking on the radio and more praying for you folks, especially the ones of you I don't see that often.

"I come before you today, and I tell you I'm sorry for the way I've acted toward you."

Pastor Karlsen went silent for a moment. He bowed his head as if in prayer. I did not know what to do. The altar seemed too far and the arms of my wife too near.

In the midst of the indecision and the incredible silence of God, I heard a noise, a whisper to my right. It was my son.

"Deesus," he whispered. "Dank-oo, Deesus."

Epilogue

Everything did not come up roses for Hartville. Deacon Wright was in such disagreement with Pastor Karlsen that he left the church and took a few disgruntled members with him. A month later he started his own program on the Christian station, and his most repeated phrase was "We're not selling out like some people."

Betty Stanton experienced a real change, but her zeal was not according to knowledge. She hounded the music director of the church until he relented and allowed her to sing during an offertory one Sunday.

She wore a pink jumpsuit with bubble sunglasses. She didn't have sideburns, but she did take the microphone and swing it in big loops, almost hitting Pastor Karlsen in the head.

Then she sang:

You ain't nothin' but a sinner,
Sinnin' all the time.
You ain't nothin' but a sinner,
Depraved in the mind.
You ain't never goin' to heaven till you meet a friend of mine.

No one doubted Betty's sincerity, but the tempo, the style and the little snarl she put in the song were too much for the congregation. She told me she was working on more acceptable tunes and hoped to sing a Christian version of "Blue Christmas" at some point. We're all holding our breath.

Despite these setbacks, there continues to be a new spirit in town. The City Council set aside a special corner of the City Hall lawn for anyone who wanted to put up a display the next year. It was basically the same rule as the year before, but the people's reaction was different. With the unanimous permission of the City Council, Hartville Community Church erected a permanent plaque to commemorate that special Christmas.

On top of the five-foot-tall cement block was a bronzed manger and an inscription that read,

> In commemoration of the manger that tore us apart, the child who brought us together, and the One who offers lasting forgiveness, Hartville Community Church dedicates this monument in their honor.

The day the plaque was commissioned I wrote a very personal column describing Hartville's transformation. The next day I received what looked to me like a legal notice with a return address from an out-of-state law firm. I opened the letter and read the following:

> On behalf of my client, the undersigned, we demand the plaque to be erected on government property by the group known as Hartville Community Church be denied access to said public property unless it meets the following condition. It must refrain from using the phrase "the child who brought us together" and use instead the phrase "Rob Freep, who got away."

The letter was signed, "Dierdra Bergman Freep, JK (Just Kidding)." Beside the signature was a smiley face, and underneath she had scribbled, "I guess I'll let it slide this time, Grim."

I have kept that letter in a drawer at work, and I still pull it out periodically. On the wall beside me is a framed copy of the column that started it all, signed by Phyllis, Pastor Karlsen and Dierdra Freep.

And somewhere on my desk, amidst a cluttered pile of letters and clippings, is a picture of a family—two girls who are growing up much too fast, a husband and wife who are growing together instead of apart, and the blurry photo of a swaying child in slippers.

These are reminders of the year Hartville went away with the manger. The year I finally came home.